PENGUIN BOOKS

MULLIGATAWNY SOUP

Manorama Mathai was educated at Delhi and Oxford and worked with the UNICEF and later with NGOs all over the world as a development communications consultant.

She began writing at the age of six and wrote a chronicle titled, *Mrs Pig's Washing Day.* Her published works include: *Lilies That Fester,* 1989; *In Other Words,* 1992; *More Stories From Bangkok and Beyond,* 1992, and numerous articles and features both in India and abroad.

Manorama Mathai is married and lives in Bangkok.

MANORAMA MATHAI

MULLIGATAWNY SOUP

PENGUIN BOOKS

Penguin Books India (P) Ltd., B4/246 Safdarjung Enclave, New Delhi 110 029, India

Penguin Books Ltd., 27 Wrights Lane, London, W8 5TZ, UK

Penguin Books USA Inc., 375 Hudson Street, New York, New York 10014, USA

Penguin Books Australia Ltd., Ringwood, Victoria, Australia

Penguin Books Canada Ltd., 10 Alcorn Avenue, Suite 300, Toronto, Ontario M4V 3B2, Canada

Penguin Books (NZ) Ltd., 182-190 Wairau Road, Auckland 10, New Zealand

First published by Penguin Books India (P) Ltd. 1993

Typeset in Palatino by The New Concept Consultancy Services, New Delhi

Made in India by Ananda Offset Pvt. Ltd., Calcutta

For PETER MOSS who endured much
and for SAMUEL, MARY and SUJATHA MATHAI

Contents

Preface   1

Chapter One   6

Chapter Two   13

Chapter Three   28

Chapter Four   47

Chapter Five   62

Chapter Six   77

Chapter Seven   92

Chapter Eight   97

Chapter Nine   111

Chapter Ten   120

Chapter Eleven   129

Chapter Twelve   138

Chapter Thirteen (Epilogue)   147

Wherefore set thy mind

My race, to know? The generations are
As of the leaves, so also of mankind.
As the leaves fall, now withering in the wind,
And others are put forth, and spring descends,
Such on the earth the race of men we find;
Each in his order a set time attends;
One generation rises and another ends.

— *Iliad* **(Worsley)**

*

If we shadows have offended,
Think but this, & all is mended,
That you have but slumber'd here
While these visions did appear.

— *A Midsummer Night's Dream*

Preface

I never took much interest in the country to which I half belonged because all of me was and always has been in England where I was born and bred. Until my mother remarried. No, I am not going to do the Freudian thing, delve back into the womb or wherever and start blaming my parents for everything that I am and all that I am not. Anyway, this is not my story, it is the story of another woman altogether, and I, as her narrator, will tell you only what I consider relevant of myself.

My mother is English and my father was Indian. I do not know why I put that in the past tense; for all I know he may very well be alive somewhere among the teeming masses they call Calcutta, but I suppose since I have never met him, for me he is not a real live person. He met my mother in London where he had come to study after which, having got his degree and me, he went back to India, taking the degree but not the daughter. Since then, for a non-existent person, he has taken up a disproportionate amount of my time and thought, and one of the purposes of this book is to exorcise him once and for all.

My mother had a very poor idea of where he had come from in the first place, so she could hardly, I suppose, be expected to know where he went, especially since he had somehow omitted to tell her that he was actually going. The only explanation I can find for her stupidity is that she had married him when she was very young, dazzled by his exotic good looks and his very nice, respectful good manners.

My father departed for his native land just before I was born, ostensibly to attend his father's sickbed, but as time wore on it became clear to every bystander that he was not coming back. When it also became clear to my mother I, not expected to put in an appearance for a couple of months, decided like Macduff to be torn untimely from my mother's womb. Everyone rallied round my mother with sympathy and cups of tea, that very English panacea for all ills, called my father every kind of name and made clucking noises over me when I made my unscheduled arrival with, as my grandmother put it, a drop too much coffee and not nearly enough milk. By which she meant that I was not true-blue white.

I suppose my grandmother just did not understand genetics, or that she hoped that as I was born without, you might say, benefit of father, I ought to have been white like everyone else in her family. Which is odd when I come to think of it, because she is quick to talk of things like the nigger in the woodpile, or was, until the Race Relations Act made everyone more careful about what they said, at least out loud.

For me that was a mere pinprick and I did not think of myself as Anglo-Indian, or even Indo-Anglian like the English Literature they write in India these days. When a schoolfriend-turned-enemy on the playground calls you 'blackie' or 'gollywog', or someone on the street shouts 'go home Paki' (and I don't blame them for not being able to distinguish one from the other, I cannot), it brings you up with a sudden start. But since home for me has always been Camden, that northern borough of London, a safe Labour seat and a melting-pot of races and cultures, I don't stand out really and anyway, with everyone suddenly bending over blackwards (to coin a phrase), any racialism I experienced on account of my somewhat brown skin was nebulous, hard to pinpoint and could be said to be the result of personal prejudice.

Nowadays, if you ask me, it is fairly difficult to be white in multi-racial Britain where the word racist has become synonymous with white and almost by definition never to be applied to anyone black. Where I live they say (under their breath, of course) that if one is not black, female, gay, disabled, one doesn't stand a chance. But I digress.

I only became aware of my roots much later, stopped thinking of myself as entirely English, began to use the phrase 'of Indian origin', began to question who I really was and where I actually belonged. This happened, as I think I have said, when my mother remarried. Like Hamlet, I did not like my stepfather. No, he wasn't my uncle. This time she got it right and married a white. They were furious when I made that up and sang it around the house at the very top of my not very melodious voice

2

and it was not the decibel count to which they objected. My grandmother said I lacked respect.

Like I said, my stepfather is white and no mistake and I suppose I did not like him because seeing him with my mother made me feel an outsider, their joint whiteness excluding me, making me the one who did not belong. That is partly why I embarked on this literary exercise, to study the whole business of not belonging, to try and make sense of it all, for myself.

When I finally left school with just about one A Level to my name, I joined the local poly and enrolled myself in a course on creative writing where I promptly developed a crush on the instructor. So when he suggested that I write about India I seized on the suggestion with alacrity. Actually, the prof who is something of a cynic, though quite too adorable, said: 'Why don't you climb aboard the bandwagon and write about India, take up where *Jewel In the Crown* left off?'

Well, I couldn't, could I? It stands to reason. I was not one of those who had stayed on, I had not even been there, and anyhow, it was my Indian father's India that I wanted to discover to find out what made him tick, not the India of the conquerors. But I did concede that the general idea was good and I certainly liked the prospect of working closely with the prof, so I looked around for inspiration. Camden is full of Indians of all sorts, but as I looked at the women who scurried past me in the market or along the High, scarved, booted, stockinged, their saris strangely graceless and out of keeping, looking like rabbits about to bolt down the nearest hole, I felt a disinclination to approach them. And I did not have a clue where to start.

My mother was not much help. She had married my father when she was very young and had not held on to him for very long and in the short time they had together they had obviously not talked much about India. If you ask me, she has only the haziest idea where India is. To make matters worse, she did not want to talk about the past and I suppose that was partly because of my stepdad, but also because that time when she had been briefly married and deserted was not a time she wished to

3

recall. Though she seems boringly calm and placid now, happily remarried, she must have been very unhappy then, abandoned by the man she loved, left with a brown baby. Those were not such good days for single parents, not like now when no one pays a blind bit of notice and any woman who thinks it her fundamental right to have a fatherless baby can go right ahead and have it and no stick from anyone. Quite the reverse, my grandmother says, simply egging you on with free orange juice and loads of bread in the form of benefit allowances.

To do my mother justice, all this harking back to the past and writing books about it was not her sort of thing at all; come to think of it, she and my stepdad were not keen on *Jewel in the Crown* either, preferring to watch darts or snooker on the other channel. They never read a book and the movies, telly and magazines are more their bag. Then one day, just as I was beginning to despair of ever getting anything down on paper, I went to the corner shop to buy a pint of milk and my stepdad's paper; you know the one I mean, all sex, violence and Page Three girls, that make one long for a bit of common or garden politics and got chatting with the Asian couple who own the shop about 'my book' (sounds good, doesn't it?). The woman said: 'Why don't you go and talk to the lady in 119 Morrington Terrace? *She's* from India.' They could not help because although of Indian origin, they had come from Uganda and had never been to India.

Well, I did not hang about or give myself time to think about what I was going to say. Morrington Terrace is only a little way from where I live and so I went straight there, still clutching the milk and the paper, which you can well believe, did not please my mum and stepdad when I finally got home.

When I rang the bell at 119, someone called out 'who is it?' and I did not have the faintest idea how to reply to that. What could I say? 'I want to write a story about India, please?' Well, hardly, and so I stood there shifting from one foot to the other, clutching the pinta and the paper and looking and feeling all sorts of a fool. As I dithered there, hard-pressed not to turn tail and flee home, a woman opened the front door cautiously on the

4

chain and peered fearfully out at me through the gap it afforded. Well, in Camden as elsewhere in London these days, no one but a fool would open their door to strangers. Like you would be asking to be raped or mugged or something. Old people are always doing it, opening doors, I mean, not raping or mugging, so you are always reading about what happened to some poor old octogenarian, usually attacked by some kid because nowadays the criminals are all youngsters. So I would not have been too surprised if that woman had not opened the door to me.

Before I could say anything, however, while I was still trying to formulate the best explanation for my presence, she went ahead and opened the door. 'Are youall (she pronounced it something like yawl) Indian?' she asked. While I was trying to shake my head and sort of nod at the same time, she opened the door wider and asked me in. In her rather dark entrance hall we stood and took stock of each other. She was about my colour, taller, with a very statuesque figure and must, in her youth, have been quite too beautiful. I could not have said what age she was, I just knew she was not young.

Chapter One

Her name it turned out was Elsie-Nora Ronby (and I learned from subsequent research that her people rather went in for that sort of elaborate name) and she was very friendly, seemed actually quite pleased by my stammered request for help with the book I planned to write; though I think she wondered and possibly still does, why I did not think of writing something more saleable like a romance or a mystery, set in India of course, she was well aware of the resurgence of interest in that country. Anyhow, she was welcoming and seemed happy to natter on about the past and India (she pronounced it Injya) and to answer all the questions I put to her. Of course, I did not plan to write her story right away, that idea only emerged many meetings later, and she spent most of the time that day offering me tea and all kinds of goodies and so began our association.

I realized straightaway that she was not what they call a pukka Indian, not with that name for a start, and I did not imagine that through her I was going to get within miles of my roots; but as we settled down to a regular pattern of meetings and she began gradually to unfold her life before me, I realized that we were not as dissimilar as I had first thought, and I took the decision to write about her, sort of juxtaposed with me. We were both in-betweens with a strong sense that we did not belong, and when she told me about the Sen family I could well believe that they were like my father's family; they were Bengali too.

Elsie-Nora was an Anglo-Indian, not (as she thought it necessary to explain) of English and Indian parents, but 'of English origin'. She added, though, that she now felt herself to be neither; 'Wherever I go,' she said, 'I could pass for a local, but I am always the foreigner.'

She had spent, she said, a great part of her youth dreaming of a place called Home, England, the country to which she had been brought up to believe that she belonged and doing everything in her power to get out of India, the country where

6

she had been born and had grown up, when India became independent.

'It was a shock,' she said, 'when I arrived here at last to find that people shouted racist slogans at me, telling me to go home. I thought I *was* home. It was frightening to be once more the outsider in a lonelier, more frightening environment.'

Elsie-Nora confided that when she arrived in London, soot black in those days before they cleaned up all the old buildings, raindark and sunless, she had wept. Worst of all, perhaps, was the lack of knowledge that was displayed by the people whom she met. No one seemed to know what she meant when she said she was Anglo-Indian, and suddenly being an Anglo-Indian seemed to be an important part of her identity, but no one seemed to care. It is very difficult to come to terms with the fact that what is of over-riding importance to you, something of great significance that you feel has shaped your life, is not even of passing interest to the people whom you could say had caused it to happen.

Elsie-Nora had made it back Home, but not to what her mother had envisioned for her and Mrs Ronby had seen many visions. 119 Morrington Terrace was a tall Victorian house which had been converted into flats when its upkeep as a family home became both difficult and expensive.

It was one of those buildings which once had a lot of character and what estate agents call 'period features', you could see that at once in the living-room with its moulded ceiling, its fine proportions and its splendid fireplace, but it had not been cherished in the years since it had been built. Now, with changing circumstances, it found itself in an unfashionable backwater, waiting to be rediscovered, as some of the other streets not far from here have been, in order to become up-market once more.

The paintwork was peeling and the windows had not been cleaned in a long time. Outside there stood several black rubbish bags and all around was the detritus of the street: plastic bags and food cartons, empty beer cans, cigarette packets, vaguely recognizable objects, disfigured by wind and rain. Dogs had peed over the bags and piles of dog shit littered the pavement. There were lace curtains at the windows; well, at some of them, but they had none of that starched white respectability that betokens house-proud owners.

The back gardens might once have been pretty with tended lawns and flower-beds, but now when one looked out of the window all that could be seen was grubby washing waving on their lines, broken toys and that ubiquitous plastic, caught on sad-looking bushes of wisteria and clematis that seemed to have lost the will to climb. In front of the terrace ran the railway line on which those other unfortunate immigrants, the Irish, had worked. Their descendants, drunken and destitute, still lie about the streets of Camden amidst the rubbish, and it is usually one of them, waving a bottle, who tells me to go home. 'Go home yourself,' I usually reply quite amiably.

'Well,' said Miss Ronby, 'I can hear the trains go by and they remind me of home, I mean the Railway Colony back home in India, although these trains don't sound like the good old puff-puffs we had then. A diesel train isn't the same thing at all, you know.' Ironical, isn't it, that home should always be where she was not?

She had come to England sometime in the fifties, when the laws for immigrants were not strict like they are now. Then England was still glad of coloured hands to come and do the dirty work that Englishmen did not want to do and, because they 'had never had it so good', did not need to do. London Transport actively recruited in the West Indies and the textile industries of Lancashire and Yorkshire welcomed Asian workers to man the night shifts that were needed to make expensive new machinery profitable.

'Everyone from the former colonies and all swarmed in to work as bus drivers, collect the rubbish, man factories, and they were quite welcome,' Elsie-Nora remembers. 'But nowadays all that has changed. Jobs are scarce and the dole queues far outstrip jobs, so those same people are no longer welcome. I suppose,'

8

she adds, 'I came at the right time. Couldn't possibly do it now, you know, there would be no one here now to invite me.'

Elsie-Nora was invited to come to England by her god-mother who had been one of those English domiciled in India whose domicile had ended abruptly with India's independence. She had been pitchforked back into what was nominally her own country, but where, after her long sojourn in India, she had neither friends nor loving family. As the years passed and she became increasingly lonely and isolated in London and found it harder than ever to cope with living in a welfare state that takes care of your bodily needs (if it must), but cannot deal with the need to be loved, to be important, to share nostalgia, her thoughts turned increasingly to India and to her god-daughter in Shahpur. Hearing from Mrs Ronby that the girl was unhappy, she invited her to come and live with her as her companion. Mrs Graham had died in that house and in doing so had bequeathed it to Elsie-Nora.

When I walked into that living-room, what must once have been the withdrawing-room, it seemed to me that it was still Elinor Graham's house, the house of an Edwardian woman; yet, in a funny way, her possessions, which filled the room to overflowing, were singularly fitting for Elsie-Nora. 'It's such a mixture, isn't it?' I said. 'You mean hotch-potch, don't you?' replied Elsie-Nora wryly.

Cretonne-clad sofas, imprinted with roses, Benares brass-ware, Wilton rugs and Indian carpets, sepia-tinted photographs in mother-of-pearl frames—pictures of sahibs and memsahibs tiger-hunting, pig-sticking, playing polo, the Grahams in their heyday flanked by uniformed native servants—stood around on every surface; there were aspidistras and antimacassars and English china, porcelain figurines sat cheek by jowl with Indian statuary, slit-eyed Buddhas and many-armed gods and goddesses. 'So much to polish and dust,' sighed Elsie-Nora, 'but what to do?'

After her arrival in England Elsie-Nora found employment as a secretary and spent her spare time taking care of her godmother who had sunk into senility and illness for a while before she died. 'The sad thing,' said Elsie-Nora, 'is that one can see oneself sinking into something not dissimilar, the sort of life that Aunt Elinor was reduced to, without any real friends and with inflation, less money and an awful hankering for something, somewhere, a place, perpetually out of reach.'

Coming Home could not have been all that she had hoped it would be, especially after her godmother became increasingly dependent on her. But if you think it was all gloom and doom there, this was certainly not the case. Elsie-Nora was ever ready to put the ancient record player on (she called it a radiogram) and dance and sing. She taught me the steps of all those old dances that nobody ever does any more, like I mean young people: the foxtrot, tango, samba, rumba and cha-cha-cha. She would dress up in her old frocks, as she called them—funnily enough so does my grandma—the New Look skirts and those tight sheaths that look quite glamorous, and we would whirl around the room.

This cheerful spirit is, I have discovered, characteristic of her people. When I became involved in this work, I began to read everything that I could find that was remotely connected with Anglo-India. 'It is the incompetents whom I pity,' wrote one redoubtable Englishwoman who lived in India in the nineteenth century, in a passing reference to Anglo-Indians, 'the unfortunates who have fallen between two stools and have neither inherited the thrift and resource of one side of the house nor the energy of the other. As a whole they are one of the most unfortunate races in the Empire. But,' she added, 'they have at least one most fortunate characteristic. I have seldom met a Eurasian who was morbid. Old, decrepit, penniless, there is not one of them who was not ready at the sound of a jig to totter to her feet, if only to hold up her hands to the tune and this light-heartedness must save them many a tear.'

Allowing for Lady Wilson's Victorian ponderousness, I could not have put it better myself. Elsie-Nora laughed more readily than she cried and always looked forward to a morrow that would bring something good ... maybe a letter, an unexpected windfall, or an interesting meeting, 'Like with youall, dearie. After all,' she reminded me, 'In England one can always hope to scoop the pools, or maybe Ernie will at last come up with that lucky number.'

I said that I read everything I could lay my hands on about Anglo-India and there was plenty of that, but I found little or nothing about the real Anglo-Indians, Elsie-Nora's people; it is as if they were of no importance, just extras waiting in the wings, but never summoned on to the stage where the real drama unfolded between the English and the Indians.

This, in a way, brings me to my choice of title. The prof, when I took the first draft to him, did not like my choice. 'No, I haven't written a cookbook,' I assured him, 'I wouldn't know where to start, I don't know my coriander from my cumin.'

The prof frowned: 'A touch flippant, don't you think?'

'No,' I told him, 'just light-hearted, because surely that is a treasure in a world full of sorrow and suffering, a quality too often disregarded and set aside, surrendered to greed, violence, savage rites.' (I only ever talk like that when I'm with the prof). But I meant that about light-heartedness.

When Elsie-Nora told me about mulligatawny soup, I stopped looking around for a title, and believe you me, a first time novelist can get very hung up on those. The soup, which was a favourite of Elise-Nora's, was a soup born in Anglo-India, a product of English and Indian tastes, a mixture of meat and spices, lentils and rice, a coming together of separate alien elements in an original recipe. 'Mulagu' means pepper and 'thani' is water in Tamil, and mulligatawny literally means pepper-water. The English abroad were always taking foreign words, and by totally mispronouncing them they made them more acceptably English. Indians have been madly backtracking ever since to bring back the original words, like Tiruchirapalli for Trichnopoly.

I have ended up, I who was in search of my roots, scampering through a part of India with an Anglo-Indian woman called Elsie-Nora Ronby, whose India was not mine, not the India that I was seeking and who, in a sense, knew as little about it as I did. But there were similarities and I did get an insight into the circumstances that had produced my absconding father. Now I understand that a little better, I can lay him aside and get on with myself, my life here in England, which has nothing to do with him. Two different worlds came briefly together to produce Elsie-Nora and me, who can, I suppose, be called the statistics of colonialism and all the racial prejudice that thereof did ensue. Just as the Sens did not want Elsie-Nora to be one of them, so the Roys (my father's people) had not wanted my mother. Well, I'm British and always will be, and so is Elsie-Nora now, and as she says, 'Maybe a country is only a state of mind.'

Chapter Two

'My great-grandfather was a real, live Englishman,' Elsie-Nora announced. She made it sound like she was flying the flag.

You could say that she did not choose the time of her birth very judiciously, too late for the world she ought to have inhabited and too early to make a place in the one in which she had to live out her youth. She was born in Shahpur, a small north-eastern town in India, at a time when that country was still under colonial rule, when it did not seem very fortunate to be born an Indian. If one was not lucky enough to be born an Englishman, then the next best thing was to be an Anglo-Indian. Or so it seemed to the Anglo-Indian, with a great deal of stress on the Anglo and none or as little as possible on the Indian.

Anglo-Indian was the term the English in India chose for themselves when they settled down to the serious business of living in and ruling someone else's country. They were very annoyed when the Eurasians began to call themselves Anglo-Indian as well, thus identifying themselves with the ruling class. It also confused the Census Commissioners when they attempted to get an accurate count of how many of the ruling race there were in India, and it caused the native Christians to press hotly for the same status. They saw no reason why they should not share more than just the imperial religion, which wasn't half as much fun as festival-rich Hinduism, or as egalitarian as Islam. By the time of the First World War the term Anglo-Indian had come to stand for those of mixed race, although back in England it continued to be used to describe the English who lived and worked in India.

Elsie-Nora said she had been brought up to believe that she was part of a favoured race, set apart from the Native by the superiority of the English blood that ran in her veins.

'Both my parents were Anglo-Indians,' she explained, 'and so were their parents, but my pater's grandfather was a real live Englishman. According to family history he had been a Collector, you know, of taxes and all, in a remote district where, I suppose, members of the fishing fleet, you know, English girls who sailed to India in search of husbands, could not penetrate.'

It was the custom in those days for such bachelors (and widowers, too, since many Englishwomen died young in the rigours of the Indian climate), cut off from Home and members of the fair sex, literally and metaphorically speaking, either to form liaisons with local women, or to marry girls from specially run orphanages that catered for the daughters of English fathers and Indian mothers. 'Don't ask me what happened to the sons,' said Elsie-Nora, 'because I haven't got the faintest idea.'

'I suppose they just merged into the local scene like Kipling's Kim, or Indian women, being more keen on their sons, hung on to them, while gratefully surrendering their daughters,' I hazarded.

Elsie-Nora nodded. 'Could be. Anyhow, the Kidderpore Orphanage in Calcutta was one such place where the duty of the headmistress was to marry off her charges. One of them was my great-grandmother Norah. Those places used to hold monthly balls at which Englishmen from the remote mofussil and men like my great-grandfather, Tobias Ronby, too shy to compete in the highly structured, rigid society of the day, could find wives who were at least half-English and brought up to behave like Englishwomen.'

'Heavens!' I exclaimed, fascinated and slightly horrified by the idea, 'How long did that go on for?'

'Oh, it was discontinued before the turn of the century, I think. I remember Aunt Elinor laughing with some of her friends when Mater told that story and one of them saying it smacked of Battersea Dogs Home.'

'What did they actually have to do?' I asked.

'A bachelor applied to the headmistress who carefully vetted him, then chose a suitable girl for him to meet at a carefully orchestrated tea party. A proposal was then expected the following day and when all was settled the orphanage provided the trousseau. My great-grandmother's wedding dress was worn, I remember, by my auntie Gwenny.'

So that was how Horatio Ronby had come by his 'real live English' ancestor, something not to be sneezed at in a community which can rarely trace its Anglo antecedents at all; too often there is little outward sign of it either, submerged by its dark legacy.

Only a minority of the English soldiers serving in India in those long-ago days were given permission to marry and so, quite naturally, many of them contracted various forms of liaison with native women. Though these women were, almost without exception, from the lowest rungs of the Indian social ladder, they nevertheless required some legal status and assumed that they were legally married. The truth of the matter only came out when a regiment was posted Home. Then it would be discovered that the ever-resourceful soldiers had made their own marriage documents on coloured or printed paper, the labels off bottles of beer, or tinned goods.

It was a common sight then to see angry and frightened women and children besieging the officers in charge of organizing the passage home of families, waving their pathetic 'documents'. I have read that the colonel of one such regiment avoided such scenes by the simple expedient of locking up all locally acquired families until the regiment had safely set sail for Blighty.

'Could be the reason why Anglo-Indians came to be despised by both sides. Their fathers were, usually, common soldiers or adventurers who came to India to seek their fortune, and their mothers were bazaar women, as they were called,' Elsie-Nora said and then she hastily added, 'not *all* of them, of course.'

She was silent for a while, her mind clearly back in the past.

'My mother's antecedents were more difficult to trace with any certainty, but Mater always said she hailed from Sussex and was going back there one day. Poor old Mater, she never made it, of course.'

'And did she? Hail from Sussex, I mean?'

Elsie-Nora smiled. 'No one would have ever dared ask for proof from her, Mater would have given short shrift to anyone who seemed to be gainsaying her.' Clearly, if her ancestry was uncertain, so was the lady's temper.

Home, or an imagined England, became forever after Home (always expressed with an upper case H) to those who had been left behind by the Englishmen, soldiers, adventurers, lonely men who had found temporary solace, after they sailed away to England. It was an illusory mecca to which their half-caste offspring ever after aspired. They had been left behind, but it was with an unconquerable sense of their superiority which, together with their inheritance of light skins, hair and eyes, was to set them apart from their Indian countrymen who went robustly on with their native ways. The term 'native' in colonial times was pejorative whether it referred to a person or his ways. Sadly, it also set them apart from the English who greatly feared and despised that 'touch of the tar brush'. But Mrs Ronby continued to fill her daughters' minds with the conviction that they were the equals only of Europeans and that, despite growing evidence to the contrary, British India was permanent and the best of all possible worlds, until one made it Back Home.

Unfortunately, for both Mrs Ronby and the British Empire, the aftermath of the First World War had brought about such widespread disillusionment with England that the Indian Congress abandoned its cooperation with the government, and other events that followed, like the massacre of Indians in Jallianwalla Bagh, the Black Acts of Rowlatt and a tough Press Act, were seen as India's 'reward' for loyal cooperation during the war. In the succeeding months of martial law in the Punjab, Indians were flogged and forced to crawl on all fours and it was all justified as 'defence of the realm'. Old hatred and suspicion, the legacy of the Mutiny, resurfaced and caused the first cracks in the Raj facade which would contribute to its later demolition.

'To me,' said Elsie-Nora, 'Gandhi always looked like a figure of fun, I mean to say, a bag of bones and scarcely a stitch to cover them with!' However, by 1920 he was the undisputed leader of the Congress and was the first Indian nationalist whose appeal bridged the communal gap, and he was able successfully to mount his campaign of 'satyagraha', peaceful resistance, against British rule in India.

The Ronbys took it quite personally, as well they might, for Gandhi was the beginning of the end. Under his leadership the Congress party was transformed from an élite moderate club, whose members began their meetings about discontinuing British rule by singing 'God Save the King', into a mass national party capable of mobilizing millions.

While Mrs Ronby taught her daughters to despise all things Indian, that England was Home and that the most desirable thing to do was to marry Englishmen, Gandhi glorified all things Indian and was seeking to pit his yogic powers of self-control, abstinence, vegetarianism and meditation against those very Englishmen whom Mrs Ronby sought to garner for her girls.

'I can't help seeing Gandhi as a sort of naked fakir, clad as he was only in a loincloth, barelegged, but I realize he was a symbol of simplicity who could identify with the illiterate masses and yet inspire young intellectuals educated at Eton and Oxford, Harrow and Cambridge, people from aristocratic homes. Like Nikhil Sen.'

There was a strange expression on Elsie-Nora's face, strangely angry and sad at the same time. Her green eyes were almost opaque, as if they had turned inwards and were sightless. There was an uncomfortable pause and then she continued: 'Nikhil Sen was a revolutionary, one who willingly turned his comfortable lifestyle upside down to serve the Mahatma, as Gandhi was called. Funnily enough, I believe it all began the day my pater turned Nikhil Sen out of a first-class railway carriage. That, in my opinion, was when he joined Gandhi and the Quit India movement. Tarla, his daughter, was like him. She was at school with me, but in the beginning we were not friends.'

'And why was that?' I asked, sensing that we had come to something of interest.

'Our school, the Presentation Convent, was divided into an Indian and a European Section. Tarla stayed with her friends in the Indian Section. Us Anglo-Indians and a handful of English girls made up the European Section. Oh, Tarla was a revolutionary all right, just like her father. It was unfashionable in those days to speak anything but English and against school rules too, but that little madam, purposely and rather loudly, spoke Hindi and Bengali on the playground where she could be heard by us and reported to the nuns.'

The small number of English girls tended to hang together and were inclined, most reprehensibly, to laugh at the Anglo-Indians and the way they spoke, their sing-song lilt and odd pronunciation. 'When this happened,' said Elsie-Nora, 'we took it out on the Indian girls. We drove them off the swings and the tennis-court, even those Indian girls who because of their excellent English were allowed to study and play in the European Section.'

The Indian children usually went quietly back to the Indian Section, offering little or no resistance because they were not sure of official support. Most of the teachers were Anglo-Indian and the nuns were Irish.

'Only Tarla stood her ground and defended her rights. She used to make passionate speeches, pieced together I suppose from what she had heard her father say, about what she would do to us as soon as she came into power. We thought that very funny.'

One day Tarla retaliated by slapping Elsie-Nora hard across the face and she screamed abuse: 'Your father is a Tommy and your mother is a sweeper. Nobody cares for people like you. When the English are thrown out of India (this with a defiant look at the English girls) *we* will be the rulers, us Indians, so where do you think you will be then? *I'll* tell you, in the Black Sea!'

'What on earth did she mean by that?'

'That was the charming joke they had about some of us Anglos being rather dark-skinned. I just stood there stunned, not so much by this tirade and the tight slap, nor the sight of those stupid Indian girls giggling behind their hands, but by the fact that the English girls were laughing and that they were not laughing at Tarla ... they were laughing at *me!* They were laughing at us Anglos, on whose side I had been brought up to believe they were, being routed by the Indians. It all seemed so wrong somehow, and that was when I first sensed that all was not as safe and fixed and ordered as I had been brought up to believe.' She rubbed her cheek reminiscently as she spoke, almost as if she could still feel the force of that blow.

Elsie-Nora turned and stalked off the tennis-court, trying to cover her retreat with as much dignity as she could muster. Inwardly she was seething with emotion, anger against the English girls uppermost in her mind. She knew they were smug because their ancestry could not be called in doubt and she realized that they despised her for her Indian inheritance, just as much as the Indians despised her for her Anglo ancestry.

'To both sides, it seemed to me, as I hid myself away in an empty classroom to brood over it all, that we Anglo-Indians were just rubbish. Do you know what they used to call us? "Eight annas", which meant only half a rupee and *"chee-chee"*, which is an Indian expression for anything disgusting. Delightful, no? For the first time in my life I faced the truth that I was in fact on the losing side, that Mater was wrong when she said we were the equal only of Europeans and I just sat down and wept my little heart out and all.'

Tarla, she was to discover, was generous in victory. Finding Elsie-Nora in a miserable red-eyed heap, she apologized for the slap and proffered one of her lollipops. Elsie-Nora, smiling weakly, accepted both the sweet and the truce it betokened and promised in return not to push the Indian girls around. 'And funnily enough, we became sort of best friends after that. But things had changed for me, I realized that later.'

'Why did Tarla say that about your parents?'

'Oh, that was just a way of saying that we were low-class people. A "tommy" was a British soldier and quite a bogeyman in India whom mothers used to frighten naughty children with and sweepers are just the lowest of the low.'

Mr Ronby, far from being a tommy, or any other kind of military man, was a guard on the North Eastern Railway and a good job it was too, with lots of benefits, including a nice little bungalow in the Railway Colony and the power to lord it over the hapless Indians who travelled on his train, usually third class, while ensuring that life was made as comfortable as possible for the English passengers in their first-class compartments. This meant that he was often sought out by important people who wanted to make sure of their creature comforts while they travelled and that he was feared by Indian travellers to whom he often gave a bad time. Horatio Ronby loved his work, perhaps because there he wielded power, while at home there was one greater than him in every respect . . . his wife.

Constantia Ronby, far from being a sweeper (a job performed only by Indians of the lowest caste), was the matron of the big Queen Victoria Zenana Hospital which she was proud to tell you, had the Lady Curzon Wing 'set aside exclusively for Europeans, everything tiptop and modern, just like Home'. Not that Mrs Ronby had been within miles of an English hospital, but it was what she liked to say.

Elsie-Nora had two older sisters. The eldest, Ginevra, had married an Englishman whom she had met in Calcutta during the war when she had worked as a WAC 1 (pronounced wackeye). He had been in the army, but 'Calcutta belly' had soon had him invalided out and Ginevra had gone with him, earning thereby the undying admiration of her family and the envy of her friends.

'Ginny never brought Johnny Wells back to Shahpur to meet her folks. She was always the clever one. I was on'y a little girl at the time, so I don't know what excuses she made to Mater and Pater, or even to her husband, perhaps it was the difficulties of wartime. Anyway, Mater forgave her, even though she minded very much not holding the wedding in Shahpur and not being able to show off her English son-in-law to her friends, Mrs Shaw and Mrs Broughton, and others.'

Meanwhile, she reserved an exceptionally nice bit of parachute silk that had been sold to her by a Chinese 'boxwallah' for her second daughter Gloria's wedding dress and she continually urged her to follow in her sister's footsteps. Elsie-Nora was too young then to be included in her mother's matrimonial plans, but Mrs Ronby often said to her: 'Youall are the prettiest of the three, man, youall'l get an Englishman, see if you don't and youall'l live in a grand bungalow in the Cantonment back Home and we'll all come and visit you.'

The cantonment represented the acme of perfection, for in every military town like Bangalore and Shahpur, it was where the English lived, where everything, with the exception of some irresistible tropical flora and fauna, was made to resemble England; herbaceous borders, steepled churches, palladian buildings, were lovingly recreated here by a homesick people in exile.

Gloria was, Elsie-Nora remembers, a plumply pretty girl with many boyfriends, some of them British soldiers in the Shahpur regiment. 'I suppose,' says Elsie-Nora, 'she could have got one of them to marry her and gone back Home with him, but Gloria was always a fool. Of course, things were not easy for girls in those days, no nice easy contraception and no questions asked *then*. You had to rely mostly on your fellow's good sense and anyone could have told her that Billy Wilkins didn't have a whole heap of that. She had her chance and youall could say she threw it away.'

Elsie-Nora lived in the Railway Colony, not in the cantonment. That was the preserve of the English. But she is well able to describe it because her godmother, Elinor Graham, lived there and sometimes on Elsie-Nora's birthday, or some other special occasion, she would be invited there to take tea. It is the gardens, the wide avenues, the orderliness of it all that linger in her memory. 'I don't suppose it's anything like that now,' she says, 'it all changed when the Indians took over. No planning, buildings of all types, street names changed, statues taken down and of course, millions more people per square inch, so not a lot of open space left. I wonder,' she adds dreamily, 'what Mater would have made of it all.'

'Do you mean India as it is now?' I ask.

'No. No, I mean of this place, of Home, as we used to call it. I think it would have disappointed her, she wouldn't like multi-racial Britain, not she.'

'You mean she would like England to be a segregated place like the cantonment in Shahpur?' There is disapproval in my voice, I suppose.

Elsie-Nora smiles, her beautiful wide, tolerant smile. 'Everybody has their place,' she says, 'We all can't go fitting them into other places just to suit our idea of how something should be. Mater belonged in British India, she had her place there and she saw it as high enough in the hierarchy to keep her happy. She did not believe in equality and so she minded less about being unequal, it was enough to be higher than the Native.'

Natives, of course, lived outside both the cantonment and the Railway Colony in their own natural squalor and fecundity, excluded from the clubs and other institutions of the Europeans. But when Indians began to travel abroad they realized that the cantonment, such as it was in India, did not exist in Britain and it served to add fuel to the many jokes told against the Anglo-Indian.

Mrs Ronby's hopes for her second daughter were somewhat dashed when Gloria married Billy Wilkins. Bill was well-known to the Ronby's from dances and socials at the Railway Institute and since Gloria was two months pregnant ('in the club' was how she and her friends phrased it) at the time of her wedding, most of their acquaintance thought the Ronbys were lucky to secure him. Unkind tongues wagged and it was said that Gloria's baby could be anybody's. Gloria had, in that strange phrase, 'put it about a bit', not that anyone minded too much, although Bill's mother, Lavinia Wilkins was heard to say that only her Billy had been fool enough to own up.

Bill Wilkins had fair hair and pale-blue eyes and a sallow complexion which he guarded zealously with a topi from the darkening effects of the Indian sun under which he had been born. He worked as a fireman on the railway.

The English, feeling some sort of responsibility for the anomaly they had helped to create, tried to make amends to the Anglo-Indian by handing over to them the running of their prized possession, what they sometimes referred to as their greatest gift to India, the railway.

This massive network, its tracks pushing octopus-like across the length and breadth of the giant subcontinent, became the perquisite of the Anglo-Indian. Perhaps the English were trying to make amends for their earlier, far from generous treatment of the Anglo-Indian.

Sometime in the seventeen hundreds, Standing Orders were passed which excluded Anglo-Indians not only from education in England (even when an English father was willing and able to send his son), but he was also barred from the better and higher grades of the civil and military services, disqualified for service even as privates in the East India Company's troops. Effectively, the Anglo-Indian was deprived from that time on of education, a means of livelihood, of carrying arms. A combination of motives operated here, one being the desire of the Company's share-holders in England to find jobs in India for their own true-blue offspring. The other was an irrational fear of people of mixed parentage which developed after rebellions took place in other colonies like Haiti and San Domingo, by people of mixed blood.

'It makes one wonder why we remained so loyal,' says Elsie-Nora. 'But actually, it's easy enough to explain. The English were, after all, the master race, while the Indian was of no account. The villains in the literature of British India were usually darkies, while the explanation for European wickedness was the presence, unknown till the denouement, of Indian blood coursing through the villain's veins! No wonder we tried so hard to suppress our Indian side. We were brought up to believe that

23

it was shameful, better to deny it and ally oneself with the better part, brave, victorious, heroic. The Indian side was sinister, cowardly, dishonest, unreliable.'

Privately, in their very exclusive clubs, the English laughed at the Anglo-Indian, at his slavish adherence to all things English and their unfortunate propensity to get it ever so slightly wrong. One of the jokes doing the rounds of the Shahpur Club at the time was that 'the Anglo-Indian spoke English like a native'. 'Ha ha,' said Elsie-Nora.

After their major skirmish on the playground, Elsie-Nora and Tarla Sen had, in the unaccountable way of young girls, become very good friends. It was a strange relationship if one analysed it closely, because the two girls had so little in common. However, they never did analyse it and were content with liking each other very much one moment and falling out soon afterwards as little girls do. Tarla was drawn to Elsie-Nora's good looks and easygoing ways. She, Tarla, was plain and intense, she wore glasses that, Elsie-Nora said, made her look like a little owl, her oiled black plaits drawn tightly away from her face. She was brought up in a wealthy family of intellectuals-turned-freedom fighters and she was apt to reproduce whole chunks of political speeches she had overheard, and she told Elsie-Nora that she often stood on a box and addressed her family of dolls on the subject of Indian independence. 'They were all blue-eyed and flaxen-haired, all made in England and she said they had to be punished for being English!'

Elsie-Nora was pretty and she was thoroughly good-natured. She rarely listened to what her friend said when she started to 'speechify', as she called it, and only ever cuddled *her* dolls, which were not half as beautiful and expensive as Tarla's. 'I was horrified when that young lady announced one day that she had burnt all her English made toys. I suppose we both knew that we were completely unalike, but I suppose that was what attracted us to each other in the first place.'

Meanwhile, the Non-Cooperation movement was gaining momentum, with British attempts at repression keeping pace and dissidents were thrown into jail at regular intervals. Later, the government pursued a policy of trying to win the support of the Indian middle class by granting many liberal reforms demanded by Congress. Many sympathized with Indian aspirations for swaraj, independence, although they did not all agree upon when this should come about.

On 26 January 1930, India's tricolour was actually unfurled and the date was declared Independence Day, with millions of Indians reciting a pledge which declared: '. . . we believe that if any government deprives a people of these rights (to have freedom) the people have a further right to alter or abolish it.' The Ronbys were not among those who took this pledge; in any case, it was to be seventeen years later that India's real Independence Day dawned. But the Ronbys were up in arms and Mr Ronby at least could read the writing on the wall, although he could not persuade his wife to believe that the British Raj was doomed.

Like Winston Churchill, Horatio Ronby found it 'nauseating' to see 'the half-naked fakir' Gandhi, seeming to 'parley on equal terms' with Lord Irwin, the King Emperor's Viceroy, and both gentlemen shared not amusement but outrage when Gandhi quipped in answer to a question about his attire when visiting Buckingham Palace: 'Some go in plus fours, I will go in minus fours.'

The Gandhi-Irwin Pact, announced by the Viceroy, was seen as a betrayal, by the Anglo-Indian and by a great many of the English in India, although it did serve to halt civil disobedience. Strangely enough, it pleased no one really; India's radical youth saw the pact as nothing but Indian capitulation, while the English (and of course the Anglo-Indian), saw it as the thin end of the wedge that would finally dislodge them.

'What horrified people like Pater was the way Englishmen like that C.F. Andrews, pukka English, were coming out to India and mucking in with the Natives. It seemed like betrayal, this going Indian.' That was something held in abhorrence by all old India hands.

As Mr Ronby pored over the *Statesman* and listened to his radio, it was becoming apparent to him that India was being moved towards Home Rule, despite the last ditch fight put up by Churchill and other die-hards. Then the government extended the franchise and soon provincial legislatures had Indian politicians taking office.

Mr Ronby, usually a man of few words because his wife had more than enough for both of them, said darkly: 'Bloody poor show, man, them getting out and talking of handing it all over, us included, on a plate to a damned bunch of darkies. A bloody mess they'll make of it and all, everything that weall have built up. The on'y thing that'll run decently will be the railway and why's that? Because *weall* run it, that's why. Youall mark my words now.'

In her innocence, Elsie-Nora repeated her father's words to Tarla, 'After all, *she* was always spouting *her* father's words at me,' and was surprised by the vehemence of Tarla's response as she launched into a more than usually passionate tirade. Shaking her finger in her friend's face, her eyes flashing behind her thick round glasses, she shouted: 'India is for Indians and the sooner you realize that, decide which side you are on, the better it will be for you.'

'Why should we? We'll just go Home and live with my sister Ginny in the country where we belong,' replied Elsie-Nora. This innocent reply, a distillation of her mother's oft-repeated statement, was greeted with hoots of laughter by a cruelly mocking Tarla, surrounded by her Indian friends.

'Oh yes?' she asked, shaking with forced laughter, 'Then they will ask you why you speak so funnily and whether you fell into the Black Sea on your way there. I suppose,' grinning wickedly, 'you are going to live in the cantonment over there?'

Elsie-Nora pouted and nodded defiantly.

'Well,' responded Tarla, hands on hips, ready to deliver the *coup de grâce*, 'my father says there's no such thing in England, which only shows how much you know; you're just an in-between and your home is nowhere and you're a silly goose.'

26

Tarla's tone became quite affectionate because she felt that she had scored all the points, but to Elsie-Nora her words sounded cruel and mocking and she sensed the truth of what Tarla was saying. 'I knew I was nowhere and that I and my family would be out of place in the India left behind by the English. Once, that was an unimaginable possibility, but now I knew it was going to happen and that we were ill-equipped for it.'

What most people, like the Ronbys, did not take into account was that the British, first at home, and then more reluctantly in India, were beginning to lose faith in the Raj. It was beginning to be described as a giant confidence trick. By starting to question their moral right to govern India, the English hammered in the first nails into the coffin of colonialism. The war and its depletion of England's resources, combined with Indian nationalism that could no longer be denied, did the rest.

Chapter Three

Shahpur was the town where Elsie-Nora grew up and spent all her formative years; it was a typical district town carefully divided into well-defined areas such as the cantonment, the Civil Lines, the Railway Colony, the native quarters, the Nawab's palace. Of course, these distinctions only held good during the British Raj and broke down immediately after independence.

Before the British took over, Shahpur had been ruled by a hereditary ruler, the Nawab, whose palace had originally been a crenellated fortress within the sheltering walls of which the Nawab's subjects had lived. Unfortunately, a Nawab in the eighteenth century decided to use the East India Company to help him fight a neighbouring Raja and they had done so with success, after which the hapless ruler found that the British had come to stay.

Later, a British regiment had been stationed there and the cantonment was built where English officers, and later still English civil servants, lived in large comfortable bungalows with deep verandas, shaded by flaming gulmohur, laburnum and jacaranda trees.

Here, in miniature parkland wrested from the desert beyond, stood the British Club, where the only brown faces to be seen were those of the servants, the bearers, clad in starched white uniforms, but by some strange anomaly, with bare brown feet peeping out from under starched white drill trousers. One member of the club ensconced in his favourite armchair, armed with his *burra* peg, had once likened them to brown mice scuttling about and had elicited a gasp of horror from his fair companion.

The Eurasian area centred on the railway and the houses in the Railway Colony, as it was called, backed on to the tracks along which the trains whooshed past, sometimes whistling angrily as they waited for a signal, but more often than not, puffing gently, a soothing sound that had lulled Elsie-Nora and the other children of the colony to sleep more effectively than any ayah's crooning.

The gardens of these railway houses were not as well-tended as their English counterparts further away. There, *malis* weeded, planted and watered assiduously under the eagle eyes of their memsahibs who thought that any lowering of standards would bring about the downfall of the Raj and so they laboured to reproduce in Shahpur's inhospitable climate and soil as much of England as was humanly possible. They judged that it had an uplifting effect on the Natives as well.

At a little distance from both the Eurasian and British areas, yet a part of it, were the offices of the District Headquarters, the Queen Victoria Zenana Hospital, the Presentation Convent for girls and St Christopher's school for boys, attended by the children of the privileged. The Vernacular schools were, of course, located in the Native area, along with the railway station, always a hive of activity and the market, which sprawled fecund and malodorous. Except for the flower-market, which was redolent of roses and jasmine, the aromatic scent of marigolds and champak, where in the early morning people came to buy (if they were Indian) tinsel entwined garlands and other flowers to lay before their gods and to offer in the little shrines that dotted Shahpur. Here the natives huddled cheek by jowl in shanty buildings criss-crossed by gutters where the water stood stagnant and foul. Only the servants of the memsahibs came to this market, and all that they took back from there was steeped in 'pinky pani', a solution of potassium permanganate, before it found its way on to a European table. And still they were laid low, by cholera and typhoid.

In what was known as the Civil Lines, which formed the apex of a sort of unequal triangle, stood the houses of those Indians with wealth and status, government officials such as the one and only Indian in the ICS. Here too, lived the zamindars (hereditary landowners) and the owners of the large tobacco factory which provided most of the employment in Shahpur.

Across the river lay the Hindu cremation ground, situated on the left bank of the river. 'We were afraid,' said Elsie-Nora, 'to walk along there after dark for fear of the ghosts about which the servants told dreadful tales; headless corpses, wailing demons that sat up in trees waiting to enter a human body,' she shuddered. 'Besides, one never knew what gruesome sight might be seen floating down the river, such as the half-burned bodies of people whose relatives could not afford enough ghee and firewood to burn them properly. Thank goodness, the Muslims buried their dead and they did it outside the walled city, on the Grand Trunk Road.'

Furthest away, within the crumbling walls of the old fortress, was the Nawab's palace, a roseate concoction, a cross between Versailles and Mughal splendour, now somewhat down at heel and shabby. This was where in the days of the Raj, the sahibs and their memsahibs went on ceremonial occasions, although the Nawab was only a ruler in name, a puppet of the British. Sometimes the Commissioner's wife and other senior ladies partook of tea with the ladies of the zenana; not an occasion looked forward to by either side, according to Elinor Graham, as the Indian ladies had little or no English and found their visitors dull, while the latter regarded the zenana ladies with disapproval, objecting to their questionable moral status as the wives/concubines of the Nawab, as well as their giggling, indolent ways.

Sometimes, as on one memorable occasion, it was discovered that they could be spiteful, pouring attar of roses and other sickly scents too lavishly over the muslins of their English guests and then giggling and pointing, making what were clearly not complimentary observations. 'Aunt Elinor said it quite ruined one of her best muslin dresses and besides, it meant that they had to return home smelling like ladies of ill-fame,' Elsie-Nora recollected.

'But,' she continued, 'the memsahibs persisted in believing that Indians were like children who must be set a good example. Despite the heat and dust of Shahpur, they tried to show how clean and tidy the place could be kept . . . .'

'And vainly laboured to alleviate disastrous Indianness by superior precept?' I interrupted, unable to resist showing off some of my reading.

Elsie-Nora smiled and nodded. 'In actual fact, they and the native quarters had little to do with each other.'

Even religion, which should have united, kept them separate because the church had separate areas for the English, the Eurasian and the occasional Indian, products of missionary labour, often known to the rest of the population as 'rice Christians'. The pews of the English were, naturally, in front and they were enclosed on all sides so that only their heads and shoulders (if they were tall) were visible to lesser worshippers behind. 'There used to be an old joke about this,' Elsie-Nora said, 'It was something to the effect that one recognized an Indian as a brother in Christ, but not as a brother-in-law.'

This separateness was carried with great consistency, right through to the churchyard where the English, the Eurasian and the Indian Christian had their own separate burial plots. No confusion for the angel Gabriel when the graves were opened on the day of judgement!

In the English section the graves tended to be those of young women, mere girls really, of infants and men who had been killed fighting to establish England in that far from green and pleasant land. Many of the graves dated from the Mutiny and the topmost cupola of the church, its cross riddled with bullet holes, lies there among those who fell trying to defend it. 'We always had a look at it when we went for Sunday School,' Elsie-Nora remembers.

The servants who worked for the British set up another hierarchy of their own, despising everyone who was not English and zealously guarding their masters from any unsalubrious contact with the natives. 'This, funnily enough, was to continue even after independence. I remember Robert Grant saying that his bearer would never admit his Indian friends, leaving them to cool their heels on the veranda, while he went indoors to enquire if his master really wished to receive his Indian guest, for him a contradiction in terms. And he always complained that when he invited people for dinner, the cook insisted on serving "Angrezi, English, khana", with the unmistakable implication that there could be nothing better. It always mystified him,' Elsie-Nora said.

Elsie considered that it was necessary for me to understand all this because, she said, 'Only then can you realize what life was like in those days and how it shaped people like me. It is a world that has vanished for good and all and someone your age can have no conception of it.'

She is absolutely right. Living as I do in London, I could never have visualized such a structured life, such separateness; and yet, as I look at the Asians in the streets around me, I realize that there is a separateness here too which maybe has its roots in that colonial past, even though some of these people are too young to have personally experienced the British Raj. So the free countries of the world haven't got it right yet, have they?

'Tell me,' I said one day, 'about Tarla Sen.'

'Tarla's parents, the Sens, were hereditary zamindars or landowners, wealthy and aristocratic, who lived in a large sprawling bungalow in the Civil Lines with lots of servants and every kind of luxury. The family was westernized, that's why Tarla was so good at English. Nikhil Sen, her father, had studied at Harrow and Cambridge, while Mira his wife, studied at the same convent we did and wrote English poetry. Apparently, her translations of Tagore were published in England. But all this changed when they came in contact with Gandhi. They put away their western clothes and European ways; the entire family wore only homespun khadi which Mira, following Gandhi's example, learned to spin on her spinning-wheel which took pride of place on her Persian carpet. She set aside all her French chiffons and English linen and Nikhil Sen's Savile Row suits gave place to the Indian tunic and pyjama. I remember I always felt sorry for Tarla not being able to dress in voile and lace like other girls.'

The Sens published a newspaper in which the delicate English poems of Mira were replaced by inflammatory articles and unremitting editorial criticism of the government. 'No wonder,' continued Elsie-Nora, 'that the Sens were in and out of prison and with them went all the members of their family, even their old parents. Their home, when they were in it, was a meeting place for every kind of dissident. Tarla used to be allowed to sit up and listen to the talk, which she always repeated at school, which revolved around bomb throwing, satyagraha, possible assassinations, spinning, printing and distributing pamphlets. It looked as though that group was strongly united about the end in view, but much divided between non-violent and violent means.'

Only one member of that family absented himself from those meetings and took no interest in furthering the independence movement and that was Tarla's brother, Tarun. He had obviously inherited his mother's love of romantic poetry and generations of ease-loving ancestors had imbued him with the desire for comfort, harmony and above all else, peaceful inactivity. He disliked having to give up his western clothes and he detested the rough texture of khadi against his skin. 'He told me,' said Elsie-Nora, 'that his parents were very disappointed, but as he was their only son and they prided themselves on being liberal, they did not force him. Anyway, Tarla more than made up for her brother's lack of revolutionary fervour.'

Despite the friendship that had grown up between Tarla and Elsie-Nora after the incident on the playground, Elsie-Nora was never invited to the Sen home, although she knew where it was and could well imagine the opulence within, assisted by some rather boastful descriptions from Tarla.

Tarla came to school in her own little governess cart, with her ayah beside her and every evening she went home the same way, while at lunch-time her servants came and served her lunch from a silver tiffin-carrier. 'I and most of the other girls, even the English ones, only had sandwiches,' recalled Elsie-Nora. The Sens were among the first people in Shahpur to own a motor car and Mira Sen amazed the town by driving herself around in her car just like an English memsahib. 'My mater cycled to the hospital where she worked and I and some other girls who lived nearby all cycled to school. No motor cars in *our* family.

'I had never been to Tarla's house, but when my birthday came round that year I invited Tarla because she was my friend now. Tarla stayed for only twenty minutes while her ayah waited outside for her and she brought me, I remember as if it were yesterday, a nice present of scent, that lovely dark blue bottle of "Evening In Paris", and some hankies beautifully embroidered in Calcutta. Naturally, I expected to be invited to her birthday party a couple of months later.'

Elsie-Nora knew when Tarla's birthday was because that was one of the first bits of information they had exchanged when they swore eternal friendship and she had written a message in the autograph book Tarla had received for her last birthday.

'Autograph books were all the rage when I was young,' Elsie-Nora explained when she saw my bemused expression. 'We all wrote in each other's books and filled in 'walls of friendship' and other little things that we devised. I well remember what I wrote in her autograph book, on a pink page I recall, "When hills and vales divide us, your face no more I see, remember it was I, who penned these words for thee." Corny, eh?'

'What did she write in yours then?'

' "My pen is bad, my ink is pale, but my love for you will never fail." I've just remembered what my pater used to write every year in my book, "Be good sweet maid, let those who will be clever." '

'Yuk!' was all I could find to say.

'I never doubted that Tarla would invite me to her party and I asked mater what she thought I ought to get her as a birthday present; "Remember, Mater," I said, "she's a very rich girl who has everything." '

Mrs Ronby sniffed derisively: 'Why do youall (pronounced something like dyawl), want to mix yourself up with these Indians, man? Rich she may well be, but she's only a Native when all is said and done, give her a book or something.'

"She is a great reader, but . . ." I said doubtfully.

' "Can't read English well, is it?" Mater interrupted.'

' "Oh yes," I replied, smiling, "she gets the best marks for English Composition." "Shame on youall then," Mater declared, "you, a European, getting beaten by a Native." There were some things you just couldn't talk about to Mater.'

As the birthday drew nearer, however, there was no sign of an invitation to the party and Elsie-Nora began to wonder if Tarla had forgotten, but that did not seem very likely because one's birthday simply does not get forgotten so easily at that age.

'Was there to be no party that year? I wondered. But then wouldn't Tarla have said so, explained perhaps that her parents had been taken off unexpectedly to jail? Some curious sense of delicacy prevented me from asking her about it outright, but I broached the subject with Tarla's other great friend, Sushma: "What are you giving Tarla?" I asked.' "What for?" asked Sushma.

"For her birthday, of course," I replied impatiently.

"Are *you* going to her party, then?" Sushma asked, with what Mater would have described as an old-fashioned look. But I had learned one thing. There was to be a party and I had not been asked.'

Elsie-Nora turned away and opened a book, but not before she had seen the malice on Sushma's face. 'We've all been invited,' she told poor Elsie-Nora with gusto, 'Well, everyone that is, except Merle James, Vera Robins and all that set, but I suppose since you are her friend, she has invited *you*?' Sushma could not suppress her grin which showed that she knew only too well that Elsie-Nora had not been included in the guest list. She was quick to press her triumph, 'Tarla's parties are always wonderful,' she went on, pulling Elsie-Nora round to face her so that she could not hide her face, 'This year, they are bringing a magician all the way from Delhi and there is going to be a puppeteer and also rides on a camel.'

Elsie-Nora tried to pretend that she did not care, assumed an expression of calm indifference, but she felt as if her heart would burst. So great was her disappointment, she loved magic shows and would have sold her soul to ride on a camel, that she was unable to contain her anger and hurt and tackled Tarla.

'Tarla was sitting on the swing in the playground and she had the grace to blush when I asked her outright why she had not asked me to her party although I had invited her to mine. She explained in that earnest way she had, that her parents would not let her invite anyone who was not Indian, not unless they were part of the freedom struggle in some way. "And you are not, are you? My mother says that those who are not with us are against us. Otherwise I would surely have invited you, of course I would, you are my second best friend." '

A terrible anger, unusual to the usually placid and good-natured Elsie-Nora, swept over her. 'I could feel my whole body shaking with anger,' Elsie-Nora remembered. 'The words spurted out of me, almost without my being aware of them: "And *you* blame us for wanting to get out of this bloody country, man? Youall are supposed to be my friend, but you can't even ask me to your goddamned birthday party because your ma thinks I'm not good enough even to come inside your bloody house." '

'I could hear myself, knew I sounded "cheap" and "Anglo", using swear words no nice Indian girl would dream of using and if the nuns had heard me, I'd have had my mouth washed out with soap. But I just could not stop myself and kept blinking hard to stop the tears from pouring down my face. "I suppose your ma said to you: oh no, we can't have that dreadful *chee-chee* girl here in our lovely house." And I tried to imitate what I thought was a la-di-da Indian accent. "Well, to hell with you and all, I wouldn't come to your party if you went down on your knees and bloody well begged me. Youall just wait, when I'm grown up I'll go to England, yes and to the bloody cantonment if I want to, and I just hope you rot here to hell." '

Tarla was genuinely upset and tried to comfort her, but Elsie-Nora threw off her hands and turned away and Tarla did not attempt to follow her. What could she say that would lessen the hurt? How could she explain that her father had never forgotten his humiliation when Mr Ronby evicted him from that first-class carriage in order to accommodate some third-rate

Englishman and that her mother hated and despised all Anglo-Indians and had spat in the face of a sergeant who had come to arrest her, calling him a traitor?

She had been able to attend Elsie-Nora's birthday party only because her parents had been away in prison at the time and she had not explained too clearly to her grandmother exactly where she was going. How could a little girl who also hated all Anglo-Indians, except Elsie-Nora, explain all this? She wanted to throw her arms about her friend, hug her and beg her to forgive her, but Elsie-Nora was already stalking away, her back rigid, trying to hide from everyone the hot and angry tears that threatened at any moment to overwhelm her.

In this way, politics took over that innocent friendship.

'From that time on, a change took place in our relationship which continued outwardly friendly although something important had gone out of it. We were both painfully aware that an unbridgeable gap existed between us. It didn't help that Nikhil Sen took the matter of being turned out of the first-class railway carriage to court and lost his case; the court took the view that such segregation was in the interests of racial harmony and therefore, in Nikhil Sen's own best interests!'

In any case, as the years passed and both girls grew older, it became increasingly apparent that they had little in common. Tarla read books that Elsie-Nora found unreadable and she took up causes that Elsie-Nora could not enter into. Tarla was reading (and attempting to write) political treatises, from which she was always ready to read aloud if she could find anyone to listen. Instead of party frocks she wore homespun and had taken to wearing khadi saris which she had helped to spin.

'I carried pin-ups of Clark Gable, Gregory Peck and Fred Astaire; she carried pictures of Gandhi and Subhas Chandra Bose! She joined her mother in protest marches and non-violent sit-ins and one day, when the Viceroy's wife came to visit the school, Tarla refused to offer her a bouquet and because she would not agree to curtsey, had to be asked to stay away from school that day. I presented the bouquet to the Vicereine and led the school guard of honour.'

Elsie-Nora was discovering boys, dances and romance and so she had even less patience than usual with Tarla's political spoutings, politics bored and dismayed her. When Tarla expatiated, as she increasingly did, on the India they would rebuild when the English had gone, Elsie-Nora wondered what India would be like without the British and she did not want to imagine it.

She was usually slow to anger, but sometimes a fuse ignited and she would feel the need to ruffle Tarla's complacence. 'What did India have before the English got here?' she asked in a heckling voice that Tarla might have been proud of. 'It is they who built the roads, the bridges, schools and universities and taught *you* English so that youall can talk like you do now. Otherwise you would on'y be jabbering away in your silly lingo and nobody would understand a word you were saying.' As a Bengali who firmly believes that theirs is the sweetest language in the world, Tarla could be counted upon to lose her temper very thoroughly at this point.

Despite all this, a thread of very genuine friendship continued to run through their relationship and Tarla never ceased to try and bring Elsie-Nora round to her point of view, always warning her that it might soon be too late to change sides and become a 'real Indian', as she put it. 'I think she sort of felt that I might be guillotined or something, as in the French Revolution which we were reading about!'

Nevertheless, their paths were diverging and both girls knew it, dimly regretting the inevitability of their estrangement.

'I never told Tarla and I had not mentioned it to Sushma, but I had bought for Tarla's birthday a beautiful string of multi-coloured beads, all the colours of the rainbow and had it wrapped in pretty silver ribbon, tied with Mater's best bow, kept at the very back of my school desk. I knew that it had all ended, really, when I took those beads out of there, where I had thrust them out of sight, took them back home and gave them to my servant Mary.'

Elsie-Nora had begun experimenting with boys; she went to dances at the Railway Institute and to socials at the Anglo-Indian Club, where her amazing good looks and rapidly burgeoning body made her an instant success with the opposite sex. It was with pity, tinged with contempt, that she looked then at Tarla in her dreary clothes, pigtails hanging down her back, while she herself had just bobbed her hair and everybody said she looked just like Hedy Lamarr. Tarla never went out with boys, her parents did not permit it, so she could not be expected to know the thrill of being admired and having boys begging for favours.

'Anyway, *she* preferred boring old political meetings, listening to Nehru and Maulana Abul Kalam Azad and all and always spouting something that Sarojini Naidu had said.'

Elsie-Nora, as she sat kissing and canoodling (dreadful word) with Keith, or Brian, or Leslie, removing for the hundredth time their questing hands from parts of her body that had been implicitly declared no-go areas, knew that there was now nothing in common with Tarla; she had remained a child and Elsie-Nora had entered the grown-up world.

'Always in the background, like one of those eternal Greek choruses, was my mater's voice telling me to find myself an English husband before it was too late. "Don't you be a fool, man, like your sister Gloria," Mater kept saying, "Did I or did I not tell her Billy was not up to much? But, oh no, she had to go and marry Lavinia Wilkins's only son, more fool she. Now don't you go and jump in that ditch." '

'What was that about Lavinia Wilkins?' I asked. Elsie-Nora laughed. 'Lavinia Wilkins was one of those Madrasi Anglo-Indians, you know, very dark-skinned, the kind Tarla meant when she talked of falling in the Black Sea. Mater didn't like her and did not really approve of Billy.'

With her mother's exhortations always at the back of her mind and the ever present knowledge that she must not allow herself to be trapped by pregnancy as Gloria had been,

Elsie-Nora never permitted any boy, not even her favourite Keith, to 'go all the way'.

In the bushes behind the Railway Institute where courting couples snuggled together in ill-lit privacy, escaping from the ballroom where to the strains of Victor Sylvester's music they had let their emotions rise to a pitch that needed release, Elsie-Nora went with one or other of her many admirers. Some were allowed to remove her brassiere and she watched with interest as under their eager ministrations of hands and lips, her nipples rose and she tingled expectantly down below. But to no avail. She did permit some specially handsome boy like Reggie Green, who was everybody's heartthrob, to remove her knickers also, but apart from a groping finger or an eager mouth, no entrance was permitted.

'It wasn't easy, man, I was just a normal girl and I desired what I did not allow. You kids with your pill and coils and diaphragms just handed out to you, have no idea what our lot had to go through to avoid getting into trouble. I knew that pregnancy would mean marriage and that would mean being trapped forever in India, in a life bogged down by ordinariness. None of the boys I went out with were more than clerks or mechanics. Oh yes, they were all good with their hands,' she smiled wryly at her joke, 'rather than with their minds and I wanted more, much more than, say, my sister Gloria had.'

Gloria already had three children, had grown stout and coarse and complaining. Billy did not bring home enough money for his rapidly increasing family, had taken to drink and his hands shook and the tip of his nose was an ominous red. Gloria tried to supplement the family income by making chutneys and pickles which she sold from house to house in the cantonment. Since, however, she was careless and easygoing, Elsie-Nora calls her feckless, the pickles and preserves did not always get made in time and the Wilkinses were always borrowing from family and friends, loans that Elsie-Nora says, were rarely returned.

'*I* was not going to put up with that kind of life or a man like Billy for my husband.' Elsie-Nora is vehement, even after all

40

these years. Her mother had made her believe that she had the looks to buy herself into something much, much better.

By the time Elsie-Nora left school, Indian independence was no longer a faraway possibility. It was right there, right round the corner, although people like Winston Churchill, Clement Attlee and Horatio Ronby were heard to say that India would be plunged into chaos as soon as the English departed. It looked as if they might be right as Gandhi, Jinnah, Nehru and Patel attempted to hammer out the conditions of independence, when it seemed that the Muslim leader would accept nothing that the Hindus proposed, because he did not trust them to give Muslims a fair share of the bargain.

It was the beginning of a power struggle that was to end only with the country being riven in two and much later, again into three and now, if one is to believe all one reads, into several more parts.

'Pater always said and nobody listened, that India never was one country until the English took it over and made it into one. "Now, when they leave, God help us, it will be back to many little countries again and lord help us poor buggers caught in between." That's what poor old Pater always said,' declared Elsie-Nora.

Midnight meetings were held in Whitehall, in Delhi and in Karachi and no consensus seemed to emerge. But there could be no doubt that the Raj was passing away and a sense of sadness was expressed by some at the plucking out of this, the brightest jewel in the crown, for it was realized that, inevitably, the lesser gems too would fall out of their setting. The sun was going down on the British empire, denoted by large blobs of pink on the map of the world, whose tangled skeins were so astonishingly managed from that 'small, nook-shotten isle of Albion'.

That was on one level, on the other, England was exhausted by two world wars, more inward-looking and found the demands of empire-keeping depleting and resource-consuming, while many had begun to question both the relevance and the morality of it all.

41

'I was not aware of all that,' Elsie-Nora said, 'not at that age, but I knew of the anxiety of my family and community, worrying over their future in the new free India that was going to be born. From my own experience at school, I could deduce that if we had so little in British India, we would probably have much less in Indian India. They were already calling it Bharat, an old pre-British name that had no meaning for me.'

Elsie-Nora left school, having passed the Senior Cambridge examination, and took a job as a steno-typist in an English company where the prospects looked good, although soon after she joined, the countdown to English departure began and Indians were being groomed to take over. Elsie-Nora was a good secretary, able to type fast and accurately and her English was far superior to that of most of the male Indian secretaries. It was not then the done thing for Indian girls of good family to work as secretaries and she quickly became the managing director's secretary.

'What's he like, man?' Mrs Ronby asked eagerly, seeing one of her instant visions of her youngest daughter in some stately English house, dispensing tea from a silver teapot.

'He's old,' Elsie-Nora replied, (George Cartwright was in his forties), 'and he's married and has two children back Home in boarding-school.'

'Oh dear,' sighed Mrs Ronby, momentarily crestfallen, 'but, man, what about the others, man? There must be *some* young unmarried Englishmen and they must be thinking well of youall to promote youall so fast.'

'They are all married, Mater, and they have the most god-awful snobbish wives, all la-di-da and looking down on us *chee-chee* girls.'

Mrs Ronby was indignant. 'Never let me catch youall using that word again in this house, my girl, if you know what's good for you, or else youall will get a tight slap across your face. You just remember youall are as good as any of them, that youall are European too, and don't you forget that.'

42

Elsie-Nora did not think Mrs Cartwright, Mrs Harrison and Mrs Cooper-Douglass would agree, but it was too hot to argue, she could feel the sweat trickle down her ribs and hoped she was not going to have another nasty go of prickly heat. That evening she almost let Reggie, who was looking particularly handsome, go all the way. His dark hair was brylcremed back, but rose in an appealing and fashionable quiff at one side of his head, what was known as an 'Albert curl'. However, at practically the last minute she pushed him off and sat up. Handsome though he was and good-natured, 'handsome is as handsome does', as her mother was always telling her. He was only a motor mechanic and having passed only the Junior Cambridge examination, and that by the skin of his teeth, there was no chance that he would rise to better things.

'Anglo-Indian men were like that,' Elsie-Nora remarked, 'not up to much. They just seemed to lack the will and determination to get ahead and were content with dead end jobs as long as they had enough money for a good time.' She sighed, remembering the handsome Reggie who, even after he emigrated, remained nothing more than a mechanic.

Reggie was accustomed to Elsie-Nora's last minute rebuffs and he took her withdrawal philosophically, but as they sat up and rearranged their clothing, he asked: 'Where's it all going to end, sweetie? I know what youall want, man, something better than we've got, isn't it? But, man, the English are going to be leaving here pretty damn quick and then what's going to happen to all our lot, eh? *I'm* scramming out of here before it's too late and youall better decide if you want to come with me.'

Mrs Ronby sniffed. 'He's all right, that Reggie's a good boy, but he's got no gumption, just like his daddy, all good looks and nothing much up there,' she tapped her forehead meaningfully, 'He won't go far, youall mark my words.' But she was proved wrong for Reggie upped and went as far as Canada. Elsie-Nora did not accompany him and shortly after that the English left India as well, after some two hundred years of rule, handing back India to the Indians.

It happened at the stroke of the midnight hour and Nehru spoke movingly of India's tryst with destiny. Neither side made any mention of the in-betweens, the Anglo-Indians. 'Nice words,' growled Mr Ronby, as he listened to his radio, 'but what's in it for us is what I'd like to know and all. I don't know about that chap Jinnah, but I don't trust that naked fakir, or that Nehru either.' Like Mr Jinnah and the British, Horatio Ronby did not trust the Hindus. The English had always favoured the Muslims because they felt they understood them better. Unlike the Hindus, they ate beef, had only one god and were good horsemen and soldiers.

To Elsie-Nora it seemed that everybody was asking the same question, a rhetorical one really, to which no one had an answer. She began to fear that she was doomed, that by not going to Canada with Reggie she had condemned herself to life in India without a future.

The next few days did nothing to make anyone feel better, fraught as they were by fear, violence and near anarchy, as Hindus and Muslims killed and maimed each other. Thousands became homeless as India was riven into two and Muslims tried to reach the safety of Pakistan, and Hindus, stranded in what had suddenly become a foreign country, sought to reach India.

'Just see,' said Mr Ronby, 'the Hindus and Muslims are already at each other's throats the very minute the English turn their back, so what hope is there for us, eh?'

Trains and buses filled with bewildered unhappy people attempting to flee the holocaust that had been unleashed upon them by the politicians of England and India, were set upon by angry mobs and massacred. In an orgy of violence, women were raped and abducted, babies skewered like lumps of meat before their mothers' eyes.

In far away London, the politicians and old India hands shook their heads and murmured 'I told you so' at each other, wise after the event. Strangely, the man who helped to carve up the country, Lord Mountbatten, became an Indian hero and when, much later, he was killed by an Irish terrorist bomb, it was

India that went into national mourning for him. 'But Indians are an unpredictable lot, isn't it?' said Elsie-Nora.

Preoccupied with the chaos of Partition, there was little time for anyone to concern themselves with the fate of the Anglo-Indian; Gandhi had embarked on a fast unto death and Nehru was accustoming himself to ruling as India's first prime minister. The Anglo-Indians continued as before, running the railway, working as teachers, stenos, musicians and mechanics. They were nervous because they had lost their sense of being protected and with it, their position of superiority and they remembered uncomfortably how little they were liked or respected by Indians. The tables had turned and those once despised Natives were the rulers, superior people with pedigree, caste and moral status.

When Gandhi's fast had finally brought people to their senses and order was once more established, the serious business of government began and slowly the Anglo-Indian became aware of change. The railway no longer remained their exclusive preserve; questions about nationality inevitably arose and those Anglo-Indians who had not fled the country began to feel insecure enough for some of them to adopt Indian names and dress. To others, like Constantia Ronby, this was a fate worse than death and she redoubled her exhortations to her daughter to get out of the country before it was too late. Those who had earlier spoken comfortably of Home and going back there, found that they did not have the wherewithal and many were actually terrified of the prospect of migration. To make matters worse, some who had gone, returned to India because they found themselves friendless in a foreign country that was nothing like the Home of their imaginings.

'From my office, all the English started to leave and though none of them were eligible bachelors, I could not help feeling that with them was going my last chance. Mater had to watch Indians occupying beds in the Lady Curzon Wing that had been for whites only and she had to work with an entirely Indian staff. Pater kept complaining about jumped-up Indians who now sat in the first-class compartments of the trains, who shot betel juice all over the place where once they could not even have entered. It was, I tell you, frightening and depressing. Everything, the habits, beliefs, the way of life to which we had been accustomed and which had seemed good to us, had been swept aside almost overnight. We were angry, we were afraid, we were bewildered and inclined to bluster, but above all, we mourned what had passed, the Raj, which had produced us and left us marooned in the alien land of our birth.' Elsie-Nora had tears in her eyes as she spoke.

They did not know and it would have been cold comfort any way, that as the English in India had found them pathetic and amusing, so to their chagrin and dismay they found they were considered by their compatriots when they went Home. They found themselves widely regarded as a curious relic left behind by time; liberals who had read *A Passage to India* found them appalling, while others regarded them as comic. Comic and dowdy, 'colonial' came to stand for badly dressed and out of tune with the mainstream. Many, like Elinor Graham who had lived off the fat of the land in India, returned to England to find themselves impoverished, reduced to a poor standard of living without servants or position in a bleak post-war Britain. The Raj they had nurtured for some two hundred years, sometimes at great personal cost (India is strewn with the graves of English men, women and children), crumbled very quickly at the end and it was all over.

'And with us as well,' Elsie-Nora said.

Chapter Four

Elsie-Nora earned a good salary; her office was known as a British concern and it paid rather better than did its Indian counterparts. Since she lived with her parents, she could spend most of her money on herself and she dressed well. Like a lot of Anglo-Indian girls she was beautiful, seeming to have taken the best from both sides; they do say that the children of mixed marriages are usually outstandingly good-looking. Being one such product, I cannot comment objectively, but my grandmother says grudgingly that this might be true if one did not mind a swarthy skin and a 'foreign look'. Then, with a sharp look, she adds something like 'handsome is as handsome does' or, more irritatingly, 'beauty is in the eye of the beholder'.

Fortunately, Elsie-Nora did not follow the usual Anglo-Indian custom, which was to cover themselves liberally with talcum powder to make themselves appear fairer. But as soon as her mother decreed that she was old enough, she began to use the pancake make-up so popular at that time and when I met her she was still wearing it.

'Englishmen would go on their hands and knees to marry you,' Mrs Ronby often remarked, totally disregarding the fact that these said Englishmen were rapidly becoming a vanishing species, 'but don't y'all take the first one you get. We'll send you Home to England an' y'all can take your pick. That's the place for you, my girl.'

Meanwhile, Elsie-Nora continued to go out with her many Anglo-Indian boyfriends to the cinema, the AI Club, or for a drive on the back of someone's motor cycle. The club, they all agreed, was not what it used to be, not now that Indians had been able to penetrate it as they had also the once pristine English Club. This was greatly resented, especially as the interlopers got elected to committees and then tried to change the nature of the place.

Elsie-Nora joined half-heartedly in the general complaints, but she did not really care; sometimes she felt she was only marking time till, as her mother told her she would, she could get away and live quite a different life.

When Gandhi was assassinated, the whole country was united in grief and shock, even Mr Ronby going so far as to say Gandhi had been a good fellow, although he could not approve his mode of dress which looked more like undress! But Elsie-Nora remained unmoved, although she was wise enough to say nothing because to most people Gandhi, or Bapu, was the father of the nation.

Always in the background were the voices of her people bemoaning everything that was happening in India, which in their eyes could do nothing right and this was punctuated by friends and relatives saying goodbye as they left India to seek a new life elsewhere. It did not seem to reassure them that a new Anglo-Indian leader had been elected to parliament.

Tony Franklin was trying to carve out a niche for the Anglo-Indian, both in the government of the new nation and also as an integral part of a country known for its diversity. He had persuaded the government to extend some form of protection to the Anglo-Indian because, he argued, they were a weak and under-privileged section of society, a minority group no better off really than the Scheduled Castes and Backward Tribes which had already been identified as being in need of special protection.

'And so,' said Elsie-Nora wryly, 'from being, at least in our own opinion, a favoured and superior people, we became no better than an Indian tribal or some such savage.'

Tony Franklin started excellent schools where the children of Anglo-Indians received priority, as they had in the English language schools that had been run by the British. Many people worshipped Tony Franklin, arguing that he gave them self-respect, but others thought he asked too much of them and not enough of the government.

The word integration was new then and beginning to be much used at various levels. 'Usually,' said Elsie-Nora, 'it meant one lot of people telling another lot of people to stop being themselves in order to become more like them!' Tony Franklin required it of his people, arguing that unless Anglo-Indians integrated themselves they could not have a part in India's progress.

To many Anglo-Indians, perhaps the majority, the idea of integrating with Indians was, despite the changed circumstances, totally unacceptable. Nor were Indians much more receptive to the idea: 'The Indian memory is long and it was too soon,' explained Elsie-Nora, 'to ask them to forget and forgive Anglo-Indian claims of superiority. One such person was Nikhil Sen, my friend Tarla's father. I do believe he never forgave or forgot the fact that my pater once turned him out of a first-class railway carriage, so the first opportunity he gets he says everybody who does not call himself Indian should be forced to leave the country. India, he said, wanted no mongrels.' Her green eyes were hard as she brooded over this. 'Well, you may be sure *that* put the cat among the pigeons because the new Congress party was trying to make everyone believe they were going to create a secular India where all barriers of caste and creed were to be swept away. They said that Nehru wanted Nikhil Sen to make a public apology.'

Some time after this incident, unexpectedly, Elsie-Nora ran into her old friend Tarla and was surprised by the surge of affection she felt at the sight of her old school friend. Over a coffee they caught up with each other's lives. Tarla was soon to go abroad to study. 'I'm going to the London School of Economics,' she said. 'India needs all the trained people it can get. Politics will be my arena eventually, I suppose you could say it was in my blood and there is so much that needs to be done to make this the truly great nation Bapuji dreamed of.'

Elsie-Nora screwed up her face. 'You haven't changed, have you? Still making speeches, lordy Moses, how you used to bore the pants off me an' all.'

Tarla laughed. 'What about you, then? You never got that English husband; you, if you remember, were always talking about Going Home to the Cantonment!'

Both girls laughed, remembering themselves as they had been and Elsie-Nora said: 'I'm looking for a husband and won't say no to an Englishman, if you can find me one.'

'Still determined not to give in and be Indian? I suppose the thought of being free and in our own country at last doesn't excite you?'

'No, quite frankly, it doesn't,' answered Elsie-Nora. 'I grew up thinking of myself as non-Indian, Eurasian if you like, and y'all didn't hesitate to rub it in, you know, "*chee-chee*" and all that. It's your India, Tarla, not mine. We thought we were free when the English were here, but now we are under Indian rule and from where I'm standing so far it doesn't look too bright.' She looked at Tarla for a moment before adding: 'To you, after all, we all are just mongrels to be got rid of.'

Tarla blushed and did not say anything for a moment, thoughtfully sipping her coffee. Then she said: 'You know, I think it's an awful shame and I am going to do something about it.' She smiled at Elsie-Nora's satirical look, but continued doggedly: 'When I think of how many generations of Indians have grown up under British rule hardly knowing who they are, it makes me sick! We are all just in-betweens because we have lost our Indianness and we can not claim to be western either. Each one of us is a hotch-potch person, us products of British education. We think of ourselves as inferior because for about two centuries it has been drummed into us that we are. We use a foreign language with all its foreign value systems, its literature, to express our Indian selves and it does not suit us, not to mention putting us at a disadvantage. When,' Tarla continued, obviously warming to her theme, 'I read a book, who do I identify with? The Anglo-Saxon hero, not the darkies, whoever they may be. We have taken on their likes and dislikes, their enemies are our enemies.'

'Then why are y'all off to England, m'n? You should be at Benares Hindu University.'

'You mean Varanasi. You are right,' responded Tarla, 'but it's too late. I'm in a world where I stand to gain more from the

LSE, besides, my Sanskrit wouldn't be up to it. But that's exactly what I'm getting at. We need to find ourselves again, to ask ourselves who we are. We cannot go back but we do need to discover ourselves and while we are about it, we should ask why Britain was able to rule us so easily and denigrate our culture and our traditions so easily. They could not even get a foothold in countries like Afghanistan and Thailand.'

Elsie-Nora threw up her hands in submission, but Tarla continued doggedly: 'Now here's you, living like an outsider in what should be your own country and you despise the greater part of yourself because you have been taught that the only worthwhile part of you is your little Anglo bit. Doesn't that seem ridiculous to you?'

'No, it doesn't,' Elsie-Nora responded, 'I don't know anything about my Indian part, I've grown up with that "little Anglo bit".'

Tarla was not to be put off, however. The pigtails and the thick-lensed glasses might have disappeared but her crusading spirit was unchanged.

'If we Indians have failed to make you feel a part of this country where, after all, you were born and bred, then we have not created the India of our dreams.' Impulsively she leaned forward and put her hand on Elsie-Nora's, saying winningly: 'Look, why don't you come to my house tonight? I'm having a party, all young people.'

Elsie-Nora had been smiling tolerantly as she listened to her old friend, thinking how little really she had changed from the sententious child of their schooldays, despite her grown up appearance, but then her smile died and she withdrew her hand saying coldly: 'Like that birthday party of yours, do you mean?'

Tarla blushed again. 'Oh,' she said uncomfortably, 'Look, that was a long time ago; I said then I was sorry, but we were only kids and my mother had the final say. It's different now.'

'Is it?' Elsie-Nora could not help pressing the matter, probing an old wound, for childhood hurts often lie unhealed just below the surface. 'I'm still that Anglo-Indian girl, she's still your mother. To your parents I'm just an Anglo-Indian, a mongrel, your father would say, why would I be welcome now in a house where I was not welcome as a child?'

'It is different,' Tarla insisted, 'For one thing, we are grown up and,' with a smile, 'both we and India are independent now.'

Again she reached for Elsie-Nora's hand: 'I promise Elsie, you will be welcome and made to *feel* welcome. Please come for my sake. Please?'

Elsie-Nora smiled good-naturedly: 'Very well then, I'll come.'

That evening she dressed with special care, aware that she must not use too much make-up nor wear anything flashy. The Sens were a rich and cultured family and they were now reaping the rewards of their earlier nationalism in prestige and position. She must avoid in any way looking 'cheap', an adjective, she knew, frequently used by Indians to describe Anglo-Indians.

When Elsie-Nora arrived at the Sen bungalow, a long white-washed house set back from the road in a large garden, its privacy further augmented by deep verandas, she remembered how as a child she had so longed to be invited there for Tarla's birthday party and for a moment felt again the sense of hurt and anger that she had experienced at being excluded. Now, standing outside the front door, salaamed by the man at the gate and by the uniformed servants who ushered her in, she squared her shoulders in unconscious defiance, lifted her chin and strode into the drawing-room.

There were several young people gathered there in groups, nearly all of them Indians, the women beautifully dressed and bejewelled, the men smart in western evening dress or wearing the *achkan* made fashionable by Prime Minister Nehru. The Indian women were all in saris and sported heavy jewellery of the kind that today is called 'ethnic'. On their foreheads, like a third eye, a vermilion spot was placed.

Everyone turned to look at her as Elsie-Nora made her entrance and for a moment she experienced a sense of blind panic as she felt their eyes upon her. Suddenly the black lace dress, run up from a pattern out of Woman's Weekly by Singhji, the old durzi, tailor, no longer seemed as sophisticated as it had at home, admired by Mrs Ronby and the faithful Mary. She half turned as if to run out of the room, but a waiter barred the way, offering drinks from a silver salver.

'Oh there you are, Elsie,' Tarla had come up and put an affectionate arm about her, 'What will you drink?'

Tarla looked quite glamorous, her hair drawn back in a chignon, slim in a black chiffon sari. Elsie-Nora, noticing that she held in her hand a glass of *nimbu pani*, lime juice, hesitated before deciding that she needed a bit of Dutch courage.

'I'll have a gimlet, please,' she said firmly.

Armed with her drink from which she took a hasty swig to give herself courage, Elsie-Nora followed Tarla into the room. She wondered where Tarla's parents were but did not like to ask and was not sure that she really wanted to come face to face with the redoubtable Nikhil Sen.

'Come and meet my old school friend Elsie-Nora Ronby,' Tarla was saying to a group of people. 'Hey, Sushma, don't you remember Elsie?'

Sushma Puri came up and smiled pleasantly enough although she had been unable to hide her surprise at seeing Elsie-Nora there. 'I would never have recognized you,' she said, 'if Tarla had not said who you are, you look very beautiful.' Then, curiosity evident in her voice, she added: 'I never imagined Tarla still kept up with you.'

'We met again for the first time today.' Elsie-Nora thought Sushma too looked different, quite matronly, running to fat.

'Youall also look different, I did not recognize you either.'

'I'm married and have a son and I'm going to have another baby,' Sushma said proudly. A man joined them and Sushma said: 'This is my husband Rakesh Malhotra. This is Elsie-Nora Ronby who was at school with Tarla and me,' she told her husband.

Elsie-Nora did not like at all the up and down look that Mr Malhotra bestowed upon her; there was something about it that suggested he was looking over merchandise that had been offered to him, merchandise that was clearly attractive to him. Indian men, Elsie-Nora had noticed, often tended to look at her like that.

'Would you care to dance . . . er?' he asked.

'Miss Ronby,' Elsie-Nora's voice was cool, 'no, thank you, not yet, I've just arrived.'

'Come and dance with *me*, Raki,' and Sushma, who had not missed the way her husband had looked at Elsie-Nora, dragged her reluctant husband proprietorially away.

Elsie-Nora stood alone on the fringe of a group that had swallowed up Tarla and looked around her, sipping reflectively from her drink.

'Hullo,' a voice said behind her, 'you must be the Elsie-Nora Tarla spoke of.' It was a nice voice with a faint tendency to roll the 'a' into a soft round 'o'. Elsie-Nora turned to find an attractive young man smiling at her. His expression was open and friendly.

'Yes, I am,' she smiled back, 'and you?'

'I, for my sins, am Tarla's big brother, but only just, for only eleven months divide us and she is such a little bully that you could easily be deceived into thinking she was my *didi*, you know, big sister. My name is Tarun.' He held out his hand to grasp hers and shook it firmly.

'Nice to meet you,' murmured Elsie-Nora, while she tried to remember what Tarla had told her about her brother.

Tarun Sen did not immediately relinquish her hand, instead he tucked it under his arm and led her off to a quiet corner. 'Let's have a nice chat and get acquainted. You tell me all about yourself and my sister at school. I gather you and she had some ding-dong battles back then.'

Elsie-Nora was covered in confusion, recalling how she had ordered Tarla off the tennis-court. 'She was a great freedom fighter,' she said non-commitally.

'That's my whole family for you,' Tarun put out his hands expressively. 'Except me. I'm too lazy to take up causes, no matter how worthy, they are just too exhausting and life is too short to exhaust oneself like that. I used to get tired just watching my near and dear bouncing in and out of jail and organizing demos.' As he spoke he looked at her with open admiration in his soft brown eyes. 'Gosh!' he exclaimed, suddenly and boyishly, 'you are very beautiful, Elsie-Nora, but I bet you've been told that hundreds of times.'

'Never so nicely,' she replied and she meant it. There was something innocent and ingenuous about Tarla's brother.

'Come on,' he said boyishly, 'let's go and dance.' He took the drink from her hand, placed it on a nearby table and led her to a space where the carpet had been rolled back in preparation for dancing.

As they swung into the rhythm of a foxtrot, Elsie-Nora glanced around her. The room was beautifully appointed with fine furniture, Persian rugs, paintings that looked to her inexperienced eye very much like expensive originals.

'You have a lovely house,' she said. 'Where are your parents?'

'My parents? Oh, they have gone to some friends for dinner and cleared the decks for us young people. The condition being that I keep an eye on my young sister and see that no one steps out of line.' Tarun placed his face against hers and for some time they danced dreamily cheek to cheek.

Elsie-Nora caught sight of Tarla across the room and intercepted a look on her face that was worried and abstracted.

'Your sister looks worried about something,' she said to Tarun.

'Does she?' murmured Tarun, 'That's too bad,' he drew her closer and said: 'You smell so nice. Gosh, I bet all the chaps in this room are dying of jealousy.'

Elsie-Nora smiled, he was so sweet, she thought. 'What do you do, Tarun?' she asked, 'apart, that is, from not being a freedom fighter?'

Tarun grinned: 'I'm at Cambridge enjoying myself and allegedly getting a degree. I'm here for the long vac.'

As the evening progressed Elsie-Nora danced with several other men, including Sushma's husband, whom she found inclined to be amorous, even though his wife's eyes followed him reproachfully round the room. Always waiting to retrieve her was Tarun who then bore her triumphantly away and Elsie-Nora found him a welcome change from the others whose eyes were too bold, their hands too restless. One or two of them had quite openly propositioned her and she felt insulted because she did not think they treated their Indian partners similarly. All of them seemed surprised by their lack of success with her, as if she ought to have been flattered by their interest. Tarun was different. He was kind and gentle and there was nothing unpleasant about his obvious admiration and pleasure in her company.

In one corner of the spacious room, the non-dancers had assembled and at the centre of that group was Tarla, deep in animated discussion. As Elsie-Nora and Tarun danced towards them, she was able to make out that they were talking politics.

'Hey, Tar,' Tarun called to his sister, 'Why don't you stop talking and do some dancing? Jagdish *dada*,' he addressed the man standing beside Tarla, 'come on, take the floor, this music is really good.'

As they swung away from the group, Elsie-Nora asked who the man was. 'The man standing next to Tarla, with the glasses.'

'That's Dr Bannerji, Jagdish. We got into the habit when we were children of calling him *dada*, you know, big brother, because he's a bit older than us. Very good chap, but awfully serious, not like yours truly at all. He's full of ideas and profound thoughts and one of these days, if he doesn't head the London School of Economics, then he will probably become a Fellow at Cambridge or somewhere. Tarla has always adored him and both our families are hoping that one day they will make a match of it.'

Jagdish *dada*, or Dr Bannerji, looked an owlish sort of person whose eyes swam behind the thick lens of his glasses like demented fish. Finding herself beside him at dinner, Elsie-Nora attempted to make conversation by praising the lavish spread of food before them, but it soon became apparent that this was going to be an uphill task, for Dr Bannerji seemed unaware of that staple of parties, small talk. Elsie-Nora was made painfully aware of her ignorance of all the many subjects that he seemed to find fascinating and sometimes she fancied he looked at her strangely as if he wanted to put her under a microscope. She could not help feeling both relieved and aggrieved when he turned to his other neighbour and launched eloquently into speech about something to do with the linguistic reorganization of India.

'Greek to me,' she said ruefully to Tarun when he bore her away to dance.

Elsie-Nora confessed to Tarun that what she found boring or incomprehensible, or both, were clearly subjects of absorbing interest to most of the others. 'Half the time,' she said wryly, 'I'm not even sure what they all are talking about.'

'Me neither,' Tarun said promptly and cheerfully, 'that's why we two should stick together.' They both laughed and thereafter they danced together in companionable silence.

Before she left the house that night, Tarun had extracted from Elsie-Nora the telephone number at her office. 'I shall ring you tomorrow. I know you like films and there's a good one starting at the Plaza tomorrow for which I shall get tickets. You will come, won't you and then maybe we could have dinner somewhere?'

Elsie-Nora smiled and agreed. There was something so nice about Tarun, she thought, nor for the first time, he was so obviously a gent (to borrow a word from her mother), not pushy or aggressive, not needing to be slapped down as so many men in her experience did.

'Yes,' thought Elsie-Nora as she went home, 'I'll be very glad to go out with Tarun Sen. He's good-looking, he's rich and he is so *nice*.' It was an added interest that he was Indian. Elsie-Nora had never dated an Indian before.

Elsie-Nora opened her front door to find her mother lying on the settee, having her legs massaged by the faithful Mary.

'My poor legs are killing me,' said Mrs Ronby, 'I have to be after those nurses all the time, cutting corners otherwise, the lot of them. Well, my girl, did y'all have a good time?'

'Very good, Mater, a lovely party and what a posh house an' all, you should just see it, Mater.'

Mrs Ronby sniffed. 'All Indians there, I suppose,' she said indifferently.

'Very rich peoples, Sen peoples,' put in Mary, rocking back on her heels to squat on the floor. Though a Tamil and as black as the proverbial ace of spades, she thought of herself as 'yuropane' and spoke only in English to her employers. She smiled so widely that it looked as if her betel-stained teeth might split her face in two. 'Father he big mans in the Indian government, very rich mans, plenty money, plenty influences.' She nodded sagely as she imparted this information.

'Stop grinning like the Cheshire cat and bugger off to bed,' said Mrs Ronby dispassionately. 'They all are just jumped-up Natives and they wouldn't be where they are if *I* had my way.' She groaned as she struggled up from the settee and went to bed.

The next morning, no sooner had Elsie-Nora got into her office than Tarla rang. 'I hope you enjoyed the party?' she asked.

'It was lovely, Tarla, thank you ever so much for asking me an' all.'

'A lot of people there said how beautiful you are,' Tarla went on, 'It quite surprised me that even Jagdish *dada* said so, he doesn't usually notice such things.' Was there an odd undertone there, Elsie-Nora wondered, but Tarla continued before Elsie-Nora could comment: 'And of course, Tarun was quite smitten.'

'He's very nice, your brother, he looked after me so that I did not feel out of place among all those strangers an' all.'

'Oh yes,' agreed Tarla, 'he is very nice and kind. The only trouble is my brother hasn't got an ounce of ambition, but we are hoping all that will change when he gets married, which will probably be very soon. My mother wants him safely tied up before he returns to Cambridge because he's too susceptible to pretty faces and my ma doesn't want a foreign daughter-in-law.'

Elsie-Nora wondered whether Tarla, uneasy about last evening, was trying to warn her off and her hackles rose a little. 'I'm sure that's very nice,' she said evenly, 'but what the hell, m'n, does your brother always do what your mother tells him?'

'Why not?' countered Tarla, 'The girl she has in mind is very pretty, she's cultured and she's rich. She comes from our sort of background and Tarun knows and likes her. Anyway, that's the Indian way.'

'Well, I wish him luck,' replied Elsie-Nora lightly.

'Actually,' said Tarla, 'I rang to ask you if you would like to join the Tuesday Club. It's a group which meets on the first Tuesday of every month and I'm the secretary. It's good fun and you will enjoy it. It is very interesting.'

'I'm sure it is, Tarla, thanks for thinking of me an' all that, but I don't think I would fit in. I'm not intellectual and unlike you, I couldn't care less about politics.'

'That, if I may say so, is the trouble with you, Elsie. You like taking the easy way out and you should stop it and get involved.

You will meet all sorts of interesting people there and it will do you good.' Tarla sounded determined.

'You never give up do you, m'n? You sound just like you did in Standard Four when you used to lecture me to death,' Elsie-Nora said affectionately.

'Well then, you will join, won't you?' persisted Tarla.

'I'll think about it,' Elsie-Nora replied, 'but now I must get to work or my boss will sack me.' Elsie-Nora wondered whether Tarun was a member of this Tuesday Club.

The very next person to call was Tarun. 'I say, Elsie-Nora, I managed to get tickets for the film. It's got Yvonne de Carlo in it and I think she's lovely. Looks like you, in fact. After the show we could have dinner at that new restaurant, Kwality. Have you been there?'

'No, I haven't,' Elsie-Nora replied. She hesitated, remembering what Tarla had said. Then she shrugged her shoulders, why shouldn't she go out with Tarun, after all, he was old enough to take care of himself. 'I'd love to come,' she said, 'I'll see y'all outside the Plaza, okay?'

Elsie-Nora was very impressed to find that Tarun had reserved a box at the Plaza. 'In those far-off days,' Elsie-Nora explained, 'they cost something like five rupees which was a heck of a lot of money then.'

'Very posh,' she said appreciatively to Tarun, 'y'know weall usually go in the eight-anna seats.'

'It's nothing,' Tarun replied, slightly embarrassed, yet pleased by her pleasure, 'My family always has this box and the management knows us.' That had been obvious from the way they had been ushered to their seats.

They had a pleasant evening together; both of them enjoyed the picture which had lived up to its colourful pamphlet. 'All the cinemas in those days gave away pamphlets about the films they showed. Weall used to collect them and I had a huge collection of them. Nothing like it nowadays with all these videos,'

Elsie-Nora sighed gustily, whether from nostalgia for the days of films and pamphlets or for that long-ago evening with Tarun was hard to determine.

The new restaurant called Kwality boasted a live Anglo-Indian band with a crooner who, it was claimed, had come all the way from London. The lighting was romantic bordering on dark and was quite clearly popular with those lovers who needed to be discreet. Elsie-Nora, peering into the gloom, saw many Anglo-Indian girls known to her obviously out with bosses on clandestine dates.

Tarun was as charming as he had been the evening before. They seemed to share so many things in common; they loved the same music, movies, dancing and enjoyed the same sports. Though she could not help wondering when the inevitable pass would be made, Elsie-Nora felt relaxed with Tarun, able to talk easily and naturally without any of the strain she had felt with the others at Tarla's party.

'Are y'all a member of this Tuesday Club Tarla was on about?' Tarun laughed: 'Not me! I'm a very ordinary sort of chap and that sort of thing is too much like hard work, y'know, reading, analysing, discussing. I think it's far too hot in the first place for that kind of dissipation of energy. Tarla despises me for it, of course, but we have a live and let live policy.' He smiled engagingly at her: 'But don't let me put you off joining, you might enjoy it and you'd meet lots of nice people. I think Tar has an idea she needs to 'integrate' you, that you're living like an outsider and you know as well as I do what Tar is like when she gets an idea between her teeth!'

They both laughed and Elsie-Nora said: 'That's very kind of Tarla, I'm sure, but I'm like you Tarun, I'm easygoing, non-intellectual and not at all interested in politics.'

'Yes,' agreed Tarun, 'it's really amazing how much alike we are and that's why we get on so well.' He put out his hand and took hers and his brown eyes looked into hers with some kind of appeal. 'I think I could become very fond of you, Elsie, you're so nice to be with.' Then, as if embarrassed, he jumped up and pulled her up with him: 'Let's dance, they're playing my tune.'

Chapter Five

Elsie-Nora joined the Tuesday Club and refused to examine the reason why. 'The meetings bored me stiff,' she confessed, 'and I never told any of my friends about it, they'd have laughed at me. I did not contribute much to the meetings which were usually way over my head an'all.'

For some obscure reason, however, she persisted with the meetings although, she says, she thought some of the members looked at her with ill-concealed contempt, while the rest treated her with indifference.

'But I got my own back on them,' she chuckles, 'I was seeing Tarun quite regularly, (although I never told Tarla and I don't think Tarun did, either), and I used to make him laugh with my imitations of what went on.'

She did a take off on pompous Dr Bhalla in whom an imaginary Oxford accent warred with his native Punjabi intonation; then there was Miss Lily Clubwala in whom the anglophilia of the Parsee was hard-pressed by contemporaneity; she compromised by wearing what are now known as ethnic clothes and jewellery.

This same ethnicity displayed itself in the homes of the members of the Tuesday Club. 'Everything in the very best of taste and the best that money could buy, like in Mrs Mukul Chaturvedi's house,' Elsie-Nora says. 'Plus sofas were replaced by low and uncomfortable, hard as nails, Gujarati chairs; ethnic tapestries and Bengali paintings had taken over the walls; beaded and sequinned cushions were scattered on the floor although most of the members found it difficult to sit on the floor and they used to race for the chairs, only to squirm uncomfortably on those. The lead crystal and bone china remained, perhaps because Gwalior pottery and Indian glass could not in those days compete for a place on the highly polished table, though I do remember her proudly displaying a new set of *thalis* she had bought. Well, Mrs Chaturvedi was the first President of the Shahpur Indian Fine Arts Council. The ladies of SIFAC, as it came to be called, were a formidable lot who rushed round the countryside 'discovering' weavers, potters, artists. None of these ladies would be seen dead in anything imported or synthetic and they were always examining each other to see what treasure of silver or fabric might have been rescued from some forgotten village.'

As they laughed together, it seemed to both Tarun and Elsie-Nora that the nicest thing about their friendship was the way they could enjoy the same things. She was seeing Tarun quite frequently, slipping easily into a routine of movies followed by dinner. Her mother used to sniff every time she saw Elsie-Nora prepare to go out, 'and Mater's sniffs spoke volumes,' said Elsie-Nora with a reminiscent smile, 'She also used to make pointed references to jumped-up Natives with nasty dirty habits, but I just pretended not to hear.'

Her father, perhaps primed by his wife, said: 'Y'all flying a little high, my girl, isn't it?' But he said no more when Elsie-Nora assured him that she and Tarun were just good friends, though this statement gave rise to a vehement sniff of disbelief from Mrs Ronby who was then heard asking no one in particular what anyone could hope to get out of that.

Despite what she said to her father, a romantic element had crept into the relationship, indeed, you might say it had never been absent and Elsie-Nora was well aware of it. What she did not know and could not predict was what might come of it. Some instinct made her behave with unusual circumspection and caution. She allowed no liberties, though it had to be said that Tarun never attempted to take any, and behaved in every way as she imagined an Indian girl might. 'I was determined that I would not allow myself to be called 'easy' or 'cheap' and that, after they had what they wanted, was what Indian men did, going on to make arranged marriages with virgins.'

What then was she hoping for? To begin with she skirted the idea of marriage, foreseeing that it would be fraught with difficulty on both sides; but as time passed and she began to grow fond of Tarun and as her visits to the homes of the Tuesday

Club members opened her eyes to the style and opulence of upper-class Indians, she began to think that she would like to be married to him, to live in style and to belong.

The Tuesday Club, if it had done nothing else, had given her a taste for good living, for a place in society. 'In India, more than anywhere else perhaps, it matters who you are. I had begun to think of myself as an outsider and it was not a nice feeling. Marriage to Tarun would mean that I had arrived, no longer the nobody looking in. And that's not as cold-blooded as it may sound, because I cared for Tarun, I liked him very much,' Elsie-Nora added. 'When I was out with Tarun I could almost kid myself into believing that I was another person, eating 'paan' bought from a wayside stall, or being received with deference by the management of Plaza and Kwality restaurant. So when one day Tarun said that he would love to see me in a sari, I realized that I too would like to see myself in one an'all. I took a scarf and draped it across my shoulder and over my head and I tell you, m'n, I liked what I saw in my mirror.'

Tarun had suggested green to go with her eyes. Elsie-Nora did not think she could ask Tarla for help so she turned instead to another member of the Tuesday Club for assistance. Sneh Bhatnagar was, like herself, a bit of backbencher, not given to talking a great deal at the meetings. When asked to accompany Elsie-Nora but not to tell Tarla, Sneh looked somewhat askance but made no comment. They went together to Shahpur's Commercial Street where, Sneh said, the best saris were available and they sat on a mattress-covered floor, reclining against bolsters, while the salesmen threw yards of brightly coloured materials into their laps and a little boy was stationed in the loft above to throw down more as requested, the bales of cloth sometimes narrowly missing peoples' heads. All the time the eager salesmen pleated and draped the shimmering stuffs against themselves, oblivious of the incongruity of their whiskered faces, as they tried to show the material to its best advantage. Elsie-Nora chose a beautiful jade-green and then sat back and allowed Sneh to haggle over the price, every now and then throwing the material down and pretending to walk away, while the shopkeeper declared that ruin stared him in the face.

When the charade had been concluded to everyone's satisfaction, Elsie-Nora was the proud possessor of a sari and material from which to make a blouse and petticoat for it.

Elsie-Nora, choosing a moment when the coast was clear, took the cloth to Ram Singh, her mother's old durzi, who had sat for years on the veranda working at an ancient sewing-machine which he operated with his gnarled old feet.

'Ram Singh, I want a sari blouse and a petticoat made,' she told the old man, 'I will pay for it myself and you are to say nothing to my mother or to Mary.'

The tailor looked at her with disapproval. 'What do I know?' the old man asked, 'I sit here all day working, I drink my *chai*, I eat my *dal-bhat* and do not spend my time in *khoos-phoos* like some people.' This was said with a dark look which brought a lurking Mary out of one of the rooms.

'What *khoos-phoos*,' she demanded, 'Who has time for *khoos-phoos* with the likes of you around? I have to watch you like a hawk to see you not carry away any of Missy's cloth in that bag of yours. I have no time to do *khoos-phoos*.'

Elsie-Nora smiled and left them to it. It was an age-old battle in which the victory was never conclusive for the combatants enjoyed themselves too much.

When the blouse and underskirt were ready and delivered to her in a cloak and dagger fashion by Ram Singh who clearly fancied himself in the role of chief conspirator, Elsie-Nora locked her bedroom door and tried on her sari. She was amazed to see how Indian she looked, it was as if the western side of her had been emphasized only by her clothes, and now fell away from her.

When she donned the sari again, it was to attend the Tuesday Club meeting and she did so with some trepidation, wondering how the others would react and whether Tarla might suspect something. She was also afraid that if her mother saw her, there would be a major confrontation. Ram Singh had kept his word like a gentleman, but the ubiquitous Mary made dire faces at her as she prepared to go out, saying with great solemnity: 'Missy baba, what for you all go dress like Indian womans? Big Missy see you, I tells you there be plenty trouble.'

'Don't y'all go telling her then, Mary,' responded Elsie-Nora more lightly than she felt.

Mary wagged her head mournfully. 'I no tells, Missy finds out, I'se be in very bad trouble. I tells, she not likes hear, I'se still be in bad trouble.' This was undoubtedly true, Mrs Ronby being of that class of people who holds the bearer of bad tidings almost as responsible as the perpetrator.

Elsie-Nora was pleased and touched by the Tuesday Club members' reactions to her appearance in a sari. Tarla, impulsive as always, hugged her and told her she ought never to wear anything else. 'Oh, Elsie,' she said, 'you look so beautiful and so Indian, I can hardly believe it.'

Dr Bhalla looked at her over his bi-focals. 'Very nice,' he said, 'now, therefooar,' (that was how he pronounced it) 'you are a beautiful Indian lady. As Miss Sen says, you should never wear anything else.'

'Well, I only have one at the moment,' Elsie-Nora said, interrupting Miss Clubwala in a burst of Persian poetry, which caused Dr Bhalla to quote that Elsie-Nora walked in beauty like the night. She was suffused with a warm glow, seeing herself merged in an Indian group and perhaps it was this euphoric sense of belonging that stayed with her and later made her attempt it again.

When she went on to meet Tarun later that evening she could make no complaint about his reaction either. He told her over and over again how beautiful she looked, 'Even more beautiful than before, though I never would have believed that possible,' he said, and it was obvious that he could hardly take his eyes off her all evening. When he drew her into his arms to say good night, although the kiss was chaste, it was very apparent that Tarun was hardly able to let her go.

Elsie-Nora's triumph, however, was short-lived and her feeling of euphoria vanished like mist when she entered her front door. Mrs Ronby, arms akimbo, awaited her, clearly alerted by Mary who hovered behind her mistress, wringing her hands and making little moaning noises. Mr Ronby sat, or more correctly, cowered in a chair pretending to read a newspaper and looking as if he hoped that he might just manage to be overlooked.

'So,' began Mrs Ronby in magisterial tones, 'here is our Indian madam come home is it? What the hell d'y'all think you're playing at m'n?'

'At being Indian instead of Anglo, for a change, Mater,' Elsie-Nora replied as firmly as possible.

'Not in this house y'all don't, not while I'm alive to see it, my girl. We all are Anglo-Indian here and if that's not good enough for y'all, y'all better get out and that's it.'

'Mater,' began Elsie-Nora placatingly.

'Don't y'all go matering me, butter wouldn't melt in your mouth, isn't it? I knew something like this would happen when y'all started going out with that Hindoo boy and to those stupid meetings every Tuesday. Nothing was good enough for y'all after that an' all, I could see. Y'all just out of your depth, my girl, I warn you and when you find yourself in trouble, don't y'all come running to me, that's what I say, because y'all just askin' for trouble and that's flat.' She folded her arms in front of her and turned to her husband. 'Don't just sit there like a statue or something, Horry, tell the girl we all won't have these goings-on in our house. I don't know what things are coming to.'

Horatio Ronby emerged from his newspaper like a reluctant chrysalis. 'Girly,' he said, 'do as your mother tells you, she knows best an'all. Y'all out of your depth, we all don' want to see y'all hurt.'

Elsie-Nora went to her room and slowly unwound the green silk from around her, relinquishing its soft and graceful folds unwillingly. She put it away in her wardrobe, among her frocks and skirts, smoothing it gently, determined that she would wear it again, but never in the house where her mother might see her.

'I wished that Mater had more sense of proportion, that she wouldn't keep on talking about Natives and jumped-up Indians as if everything in India had not changed at all. But,' sighed Elsie-Nora, 'no one could ever tell Mater anything she didn't want to hear and expecting her to change was like telling the sun not to rise tomorrow.'

However, the sari seemed to have had the desired effect on Tarun. He was clearly struggling against deep emotion, hovering on the brink of speech and at the last moment deciding against it. He was no longer his usual placid and sunny self and Elsie-Nora knew he was, however reluctantly, in love with her.

'I loved him, one could not help loving Tarun, but I did not know how to proceed. He treated me like I was made of some rare china that might break instead of like a flesh and blood woman.'

Elsie-Nora wondered if she ought to make love to him; but it was hard to tell where that might lead for it could either frighten him away or bind him to a commitment. She knew so little of him outside their meetings that she was unable to visualize herself in his life, could conjure up no picture of herself in his home, with his parents, or even with his friends to whom she had never been introduced.

Unwittingly, she precipitated the situation with one small unthinking action. Elsie-Nora had not seen Tarun for about a week when Tarla mentioned that her brother had 'flu'. 'Such a fuss,' she exclaimed at the Tuesday Club meeting, 'one minute he's too weak to lift his head and the next moment he's trying to sneak out of bed to call some friend on the telephone. Just like a man! Ma has given orders that he's not to get out of bed till his fever goes down, what a fuss over nothing.' Elsie-Nora, hearing this, was sure Tarun had been trying to ring her.

A few days later, passing the Sen bungalow, impulsively she went in. She had just bought some records at the new HMV shop and she knew that one of them had a song that Tarun particularly liked and thought he would enjoy hearing it on his new hi-fi record player of which he was very proud and it would cheer up the invalid.

The servant who opened the door to her looked momentarily surprised when she told him she had come to see Tarun Sahib, but his face so quickly reassumed its normal expressionlessness that Elsie-Nora thought she had been mistaken. He made no comment, but stood aside and ushered her into a small sitting-room and went away, presumably to call the young master. He left the door ajar behind him.

There was a group of what looked like family photographs on the piano by the door and Elsie-Nora went over to look at them. She saw the servant open another door across the hall which he failed to close properly behind him. 'Belongs in a cowshed,' her mother would have said. Elsie-Nora caught the murmur of voices. Standing irresolute, wondering suddenly at the wisdom of her action, she heard a man say: 'To see you, Tarun? What sort of young lady is this who comes uninvited to a man's house, seeking him out? Not a very well-brought up person, eh Mira?'

'Baba, that is unkind,' she heard Tarun say, 'I asked her to . . . .'

'You asked her and she comes running?' the voice, and she knew it was Nikhil Sen's, was sarcastic, 'What a very popular young man you must be. It was not so in my young days, well-brought up young women just did not do it, and we would not permit Tarla to go running after young men.'

A chair scraped back as someone rose and Elsie-Nora shrank back behind the door. A woman's voice reached her: 'Isn't this that Anglo-Indian friend of Tarla's? That child should have been a missionary, every waif and stray she wants to take care of . . .' Elsie-Nora did not wait to hear more. Soundlessly she opened the front door and let herself out of the house.

The sunlight slanted mellow on the green lawn and Elsie-Nora remembers a blur of green and gold which to this day reminds her of that long-ago day. There were tears in her eyes but they were tears of rage, of anger against herself for having been so stupid and unthinking. That, she says, is when she knew she really loved Tarun; 'When I thought I had lost him by my stupid action.' She felt she had acted like a fool after having spent so many months being so careful and so circumspect. What must he think of her? She heard shouts behind her but only quickened her pace.

'Elsie, Elsie-Nora,' Tarun came rushing up behind her, furiously pedalling a bicycle that was rather too small for his long legs. 'The servants said you had run away. I had to borrow Bahadur Singh's, our Gurkha, bike and I look a right fool on it, I'm sure. Why did you run away like that?' catching her by the elbow as she attempted to walk on, he turned her round to face him, 'Why darling, what is the matter? You're not crying, are you? What is it Elsie?'

'Oh Tarun, I'm so sorry,' and now her tears came in earnest, 'I should never have come to your house like that. It was stupid of me, I just did not think. I heard you were ill and I wanted to cheer you up so I brought some records and now I've gone and left them. Naturally your parents think ill of me.'

Tarun let the *non sequitur* pass. He pulled her close and said: 'You heard them then. Don't mind what my father said, he is just old-fashioned. I love you, Elsie, I've been in love with you for ages, I want to marry you.' He put his lips to hers and then moved them over her face, drying her tears with his tongue.

'You can't,' Elsie-Nora said indistinctly through his ministrations.

'Why not? Don't you want to marry me?'

'Of course I do, but have you thought what your parents will say? They will never allow it.'

'They won't like it, but I don't care and for that matter, what are your parents going to say?' Tarun was smiling bravely, although he probably wasn't feeling at all brave inside. He knew only too well what his parents, especially Baba, his father, would say. Elsie-Nora's visit, he had to admit, had not made matters easier.

'My parents won't like it,' Elsie-Nora was saying; she had a pretty accurate idea of what Mater would say.

Tarun was aware of a momentary irritation which made his arms loosen from about her. He could not imagine what a lowly Anglo-Indian railway official could have to object to his daughter marrying a Bengali Brahmin from one of the best families—aristocrats on both sides and related to Tagore. Quickly, however, he quelled the disloyal thought and once more drew Elsie-Nora into his embrace. 'You see,' she explained, 'your Dad and mine had that set-to some years ago and they've always been daggers drawn since then.'

'Well,' Tarun said resolutely, 'they will all have to accept it because I love you and you love me and that's all that matters.'

As if to give himself courage, he stooped and kissed her and then spoiled it by glancing furtively round as if he expected someone to be spying on them. Now it was Elsie-Nora's turn to feel irritated, why should he behave as if he was doing something shameful? Quickly she too scotched the disloyal thought, gave him a quick kiss and stood away from him.

'What are we going to do? Will you tell your parents now?' she asked.

'May as well,' Tarun answered and did not realize how depressed he sounded, 'If there's going to be an almighty fuss, I suppose it's best to get it over with quickly.'

'I don't think I can face them ...' quavered Elsie-Nora, quailing at the thought of re-entering that house just then.

'No, no, it's best you don't come to see them now. Let them get used to the idea and then once they see you and see how beautiful you are, maybe you should wear a sari, they will come round I'm sure.'

They kissed once more, Elsie-Nora clinging to Tarun for reassurance, he furtive, unable to relax, clearly unused to public displays of affection, hasty and perfunctory. They each turned to go home to break the news to their respective families.

Predictably, Mrs Ronby was up in arms at once. 'Marry a Native boy, a Hindoo? This was what all that sari wearing was all about, was it? I told you and told you, Horry, but would you listen? Oh no, y'all just want to stick your head in the sand like an ostrich. Well, I can tell you, my girl, this kind of mumbo-jumbo wedding isn't what we had in mind for you an' all.'

'They are anti-British people, what will y'all have in common, m'n?' Mr Ronby asked. 'They all'l only look down on y'all, Elsie, don't forget it was your young man's father who called us mongrels who should be sent packing.'

'Very rich peoples,' chanted Mary, not to be left out, 'very big mans, my one cousin brother work there one times, plenty food, plenty money.'

'He's out of your class, girly, face it,' her father urged.

'She's not marrying any old Hindoo,' her mother reiterated, stoutly refusing to admit reality, 'We'll send y'll back Home to Ginny where y'all can find yourself a decent husband, one of our own kind, not one who washes his backside with his hand and then eats with his fingers.'

'Mother,' Elsie-Nora's voice rose, 'Tarun is not like that. Anyway, I love him and I'm damn well going to marry him so y'all better get used to the idea an' all.'

'Over my dead body,' said Mrs Ronby implacably, at which Mary decided to moan and wring her hands, rocking her body as if she were, indeed, at her mistress's funeral. Carried away by her own voice, Mary's keening rose to an unacceptable level and Mrs Ronby said: 'Bugger off and keep that unholy racket for your own funeral and may the jackals get you.'

This had the effect of making Mary howl louder, so that the Ronbys had to shout at each other to be heard.

Faced by this scene, unable to explain to her parents that Tarun was not just an ordinary Indian, Elsie-Nora could not help wondering with a sinking heart how Tarun was ever going to be able to bring his parents round.

She looked around the familiar room with new eyes, the eyes of the Sens, contrasting it with the style and opulence of their drawing-room. She looked at the pictures on the walls, the religious mottoes, the cheap reproductions of the *Monarch of the Glen*, *The Last Supper*, coloured prints of the British royal family, of Windsor Castle, the Lake District and knew that the Sens would despise it.

'Marriages in India are of families, not individuals,' Elsie-Nora explains, 'who they are and what they have are of the utmost importance. Us Ronbys could not be described as an advantageous connection for the Sens.'

Still, she believed in Tarun and waited every day for his call. The days passed, however, and no call came, but still Elsie-Nora did not doubt Tarun. She was certain he had not changed his mind, but if his parents remained adamant she wondered if he could stand up to them. Tarun was not a fighter, she knew, his charm lay in his sunny easygoing temperament. She herself shrank from telephoning him in case one of his parents answered and she had no illusions about Tarla being an ally. In any case, Tarla had gone up to Simla to stay with a friend.

If the Ronbys noticed the hiatus they gave no sign. Mr Ronby was one of those people who preferred to let unpleasantness wash over him, he was practised at turning a deaf ear to his wife's tirades, making soothing noises when cornered. Mrs Ronby, on the other hand, took the view that what she had expressly forbidden could not take place and so she devoted her energies to devising plans to send Elsie-Nora Home to England.

Some days later, as Elsie-Nora sat at her typewriter in the office, her mind miles away, wondering what had become of Tarun and why he had not contacted her, the peon came to tell her that she had a visitor waiting in the reception area. 'It must be Tarun at last,' she thought excitedly and almost knocked over her chair in her haste to get up. She felt no anger at Tarun's tardiness because, after all, she had not managed in all this time to bring her mother round.

When she entered the outer office, her steps faltered and her excitement faded for it was Tarla who waited there for her, restlessly turning the pages of a trade journal. Elsie-Nora stood in the doorway and hesitated. The receptionist looked up and indicated Tarla with her chin. Seeing Elsie-Nora hold back, she frowned in perplexity, then cleared her throat loudly so that Tarla turned and saw her friend.

With her usual impetuosity, Tarla ran across the room and tried to embrace Elsie-Nora who, however, stood stiff and unyielding. Slowly, Tarla dropped her arms to her side. She reached in her handbag and drew out something, which she held in her hands, twisting and turning it. Elsie-Nora did nothing, said nothing.

'Elsie, can we go somewhere and talk? Somewhere more private?' with her eyes, Tarla indicated the receptionist.

'I don't see why,' replied Elsie-Nora, 'You can say what you have come to say right here. I have nothing to hide from anyone. In fact, I'll make it easy for you; you have come to tell me that your brother doesn't want to marry me.'

'You don't know how sorry I am, Elsie,' Tarla said, 'I wish things could have turned out differently . . .' her words tailed off as she met Elsie-Nora's hard, bright stare.

'Sorry? Why should you be sorry, you didn't want me to marry your brother, surely?'

Both of them were aware that the receptionist, intrigued by the strange tableau before her, had given up all pretence of doing her work and was staring inquisitively at them, straining to hear.

'Please, Elsie, let me explain. Let's talk,' Tarla pleaded.

'There is nothing for you to explain. Why couldn't he—your brother—come and explain for himself. Why do youall have to speak for him, can't he speak for himself, tell me to my face?'

Tarla hesitated, how could she tell Elsie-Nora that her parents had not trusted Tarun to see Elsie-Nora again? She held out a letter: 'He left this for you, Elsie. Elsie, you know Tarun, he

74

is not a fighter. My father always said of Tarun that he takes the line of least resistance, but he loves our parents, he is dependent on them and it looked for a while as if my grandmother would die because she refused all medicine and food. He could not hold out against that. '

There was a pause. Tarla held out the letter and Elsie-Nora made no attempt to take it from her. Tarla hesitated once more and then she said: 'They brought forward his marriage to take place immediately. It was always understood that he would marry Radhika and they have left for England. He wanted me to see you and give you this letter and to try and explain. Believe me, Elsie, I'm very sorry.'

'You and your damned family,' said Elsie-Nora. 'I should never have come to that party of yours, never attempted to cross the tracks; apt, no, for a railway girl? But no, you had to bloody well integrate me in your wonderful new India. What for, I ask you! I should have bloody kept to my own side of the fence, isn't it?' Even now, after all these years, there are tears in Elsie-Nora's eyes as she recalls the scene although she says she never shed a tear then, not in front of Tarla.

'Don't, Elsie-Nora, please don't. I really am very, very sorry. I tried to warn Tarun right at the very beginning, that very first evening, but he wouldn't listen,' it was Tarla who had tears in her eyes.

'You tried to warn him not to have anything to do with a *chee-chee* girl like me?' Elsie-Nora's voice was vicious.

'You know what I mean. Don't twist my words please, it doesn't help anyone.'

'You had better go, Tarla,' Elsie-Nora sounded suddenly weary, 'I don't think there is anything more to be said.'

Once more, wordlessly, Tarla held out her brother's letter and Elsie-Nora ignored it. Tarla looked at her friend's cold, set face and knew that there was, indeed, nothing more to say. Nothing that could mitigate Tarun's betrayal; but Tarun was weak. People thought him gentle and easygoing, but she knew her brother would never fight for anything. He was unlike her and her father. They were fighters, Tarun gave in. He was no match for their father's sarcasm, eloquence and ability to make everyone else look a fool. He could not cope with his mother and grandmother's emotional blackmail, the old lady's Gandhian resolve to fast unto death. She did not doubt that Tarun had loved Elsie-Nora, but there seemed little point in saying that now. In any case, her brother had probably said it all in his letter and once more she extended it to Elsie-Nora. This time she took it and looking Tarla in the face, she tore it across and across.

Tarla was aghast, but she made one last effort: 'I'm leaving soon for London, but if there is anything I can do for you, please tell me.' She knew her words were inadequate, even meaningless, but she did not know what else to say or do. 'Goodbye, Elsie, I hope things go well with you.'

Even as she spoke, Elsie-Nora had turned away so that it was her back that Tarla addressed and she did not see the tears that had welled up in Elsie-Nora's eyes. Tarla's eyes met instead the interested gaze of the receptionist and she wondered what the woman, an Anglo-Indian, had made of the exchange, most of which she had clearly overheard.

Tarla turned and left the office. She was sad. Although she understood the family's resistance to their only son marrying an Anglo-Indian, she could also understand why Tarun had fallen in love with Elsie-Nora and she could identify with her sense of betrayal and anger. Why, oh why, did people have to be governed by notions of class, race, colour and creed? Yet they were, she was. She had to admit that she would not have wanted the Ronbys as her *bandhus*, connections by marriage.

Well, she was off to London and Jagdish was going with her; she knew that when they returned to India they would be married. It was what everyone wanted. They spoke the same language, believed in the same things, had the same ambitions and desires. It was not so for Tarun and Elsie-Nora, Elsie was an outsider, not one of them. Tarla sighed and could not have said whether it was for herself or for her friend.

Chapter Six

The Ronbys were pleased that their daughter's romance had come to nothing. 'What do we want with a Bengali babu, however educated or rich?' Mrs Ronby wanted to know. She shared the British distrust of the educated Indian, the 'babu', of whom Lord Lytton wrote in 1877, 'The only political representatives of native opinion are the babus whom we have educated ... who represent nothing but the social anomaly of their own position.'

'They are not our sort of people,' Mrs Ronby put it more succinctly, meaning much the same thing, 'Are they, Pater?'

Mr Ronby, trying to read his paper and listen to the radio at the same time, nodded and made affirmative noises. He had long ago learned that to ignore Constantia was a dangerous and unprofitable pastime.

'Who are our sort of people, then?' Elsie-Nora asked belligerently.

'Don't y'all take that tone of voice with me, Madam,' replied her mother, 'Y'all know very well what I mean. Ginny's husband and Gloria's Billy, they are our sort of people. *Our* ancestors came from England and don't y'all forget that, m'n.'

Gloria nodded in agreement and looked spitefully at her sister of whose youth, good looks and independence she was very jealous.

Elsie-Nora looked at her with loathing. 'Oh yeah?' she drawled insolently, 'Fat lot of good that's done Gloria and her wunnerful Billy. Some of our ancestors did not come from England, that's the problem, that's why weall are looked down upon by both sides.'

'Y'll speak for yourself,' Gloria retorted, 'Me 'n Billy, weall don' have any problem, do we Bill?'

Bill was pouring himself yet another drink, his hand shaking as he tried to steady the bottle: 'Washever you say, sweetie,' he replied slurring his words and he leered amiably at them.

Elsie-Nora looked at Gloria and Bill with distaste. 'Your sort I can do without,' she said, 'Just take a dekko at yourselves, you look like a fat slut and that husband of yours is an alcoholic, for chrissake.'

Gloria's temper, like her mother's, was on a short fuse. She flung herself on her sister with an inarticulate cry of rage and began to scratch and bite her. In attempting to separate them, the whole family pitched in, screeching and swearing, Mrs Ronby declaring that she would teach Elsie-Nora not to take God's name in vain, by God, while Billy smiling vacuously, refilled his glass and his three children watched round-eyed.

The fight ended as abruptly as it had begun when Elsie-Nora threw her sister off her and walked out of the room. As she bathed the scratches and bruises on her face and arms and looked at herself in the bathroom mirror, she felt ashamed of herself for taking part in what was nothing less than a common brawl. She could hear Gloria and her mother yelling at each other outside and she wished herself miles away.

Elsie-Nora was unhappy and her unhappiness was tinged with a sense of humiliation. Tarun had jilted her and although her parents had never said 'I told you so', she knew that they thought it. She had wanted to escape herself, them, her background, had not wanted to be a part of all that, and now her loss of self-control showed that she was very much a part of it. If she married what her mother called 'our sort', she would never escape. Leaning her head against the cool wash-basin, Elsie-Nora wept.

The feeling of being trapped forever, her unhappiness at Tarun's defection, gave her a bitter need to pick on her family, to give offence, something foreign to her normally sunny nature. Nothing, however, made it any better. Her mother usually remained unmoved, only reiterating that Elsie-Nora would one day be thankful she had not married 'that Hindoo'.

To Mrs Ronby's credit it could be said that her prejudice was so unfaltering that neither wealth nor status had any effect on it. In any case, as she said to the rest of her family, out of

Elsie-Nora's hearing, 'Handsome is as handsome does and that young man acted like a blackguard to our Elsie and I'd say that to his face if I had the chance an' all.'

To Elsie-Nora it began to look as if what her mother and others of their community had always said was true after all; there was no future for her in India, no prospect of bettering herself. But where else then? England was a faraway and unknown country, Home only in name .... Ginny, her sister who had married and settled there, much older than she, rarely wrote home and had never encouraged any of her family to think of joining her there, painting a bleak picture of post-war Britain and saying they were much better off in India.

'The truth is,' said Elsie-Nora, 'Ginny was afraid that my brown skin would give the game away, show people that she was not the true-blue Brit she claimed to be. She could get away with it with her blue eyes and fair skin and hair. Like you,' she added with a smile, 'I don't have enough milk in my coffee.'

Of course, all this colour consciousness and race discrimination in England was to change later as Britain rapidly turned into a multi-racial society; 'Well, at least one can't express it openly any more, but that's the way it was in the old days,' Elsie-Nora explained. 'Ginny had taught herself to speak differently, to explain away the Anglo-Indian lilt by claiming to be of Welsh extraction. She had merged into the small Dorset community she lived in and the last thing she wanted was the tar brush turning up on her doorstep in the shape of her sister.'

People had been told so often about her being 'Domiciled English' that even her husband had come to believe it. He had never met the Ronbys and the few black and white photographs in the family album revealed nothing. 'The wife's family out in India,' Johnny Wells might say proudly and the small inward-looking village community of which they were part, with little interest in outsiders, left it at that.

When, therefore, Mrs Ronby wrote to her eldest daughter of Elsie-Nora's plight and requested her to 'Do what you can for the poor girl, get her out of this damn country for a start, give her a chance of a new start back Home,' Ginny replied with unusual promptness saying that she could not have her sister to stay. The reasons, like blackberries, were plentiful: all her children were at home, her husband's brother from Australia was visiting, it was only a small village that they lived in where most of the population were in their seventies, too old to be any use to Elsie-Nora.

Elsie-Nora shrugged when her mother told her. She could guess the real reason why her sister did not want her there and if that was the case, it wouldn't do her much good to go, anyway. In any case, she was too miserable to care.

She had tried to piece together Tarun's letter which she had so impetuously torn to shreds and had been largely unsuccessful.

'Beware the grand gesture unless you really mean it,' she said, 'all I managed to do was to make out something that looked like the word love and that brought on a storm of weeping.'

She continued to go to work and out with her friends, doing everything like an automaton. Of course, she stopped going to the Tuesday Club meetings and after a few polite reminders they ceased to send her their notices. Tarun and to some extent Tarla, had been the *raison d'etre* for her and without them, she had no further use for the Tuesday Club.

The only person who could, at least in one sense, reach her was her boss Dinesh Poddar, whom she loathed. He was becoming more lecherous every day; from merely staring at her with hooded eyes that furtively undressed her, he had progressed to leaning over her at her desk, brushing up against her in the corridor and touching her as if by accident.

'Who the hell does he think he is?' she raged to the other girls in the typing pool. Josephine Jackson laughed: 'Poddy? He's only the boss that's all and I happen to know he's Management's blue-eyed boy an' all and if y'all went complaining about him you'd get the sack.' Sexual harrassment was alive and well, but in India in those days (and I suppose here in England too) people weren't organized to deal with it. No feminist movement then.

'They are all the same,' said Ruby Thomas, 'they think we all are loose girls just because we work for a living and show our legs and are freer than the Indian girls.'

'Well, if Poddar touches me once more purposely by accident, I'm going to give him a tight slap and he can take his job and stuff it for all I care,' Elsie-Nora was still seething. The other girls laughed disbelievingly.

'You'd do better to keep him sweet,' Josephine told her with a meaning wink.

'Guess what, girls?' Maggie Wilson, the Admin secretary came through the door with a sheaf of papers in her hand. 'We've got a new man coming out from London, from Head Office. He's to head Research and Development and I have to give him our best secretary, find him a house, interview servants for him. He'll be here in a couple of weeks.'

All the girls were agog with curiosity and they clustered round her demanding to know more. 'Well,' said Maggie, 'first things first, the Chairman has decided that Elsie-Nora is to be his secretary, over the protests of Poddy as you may imagine,' she winked at Elsie-Nora.

'Thank God, it's about time I had a change.'

The other girls groaned and commiserated with each other good-naturedly. 'Trust you to have all the luck' and 'It's not fair,' they said, but they smiled and wished Elsie-Nora luck.

'Who is this new man?' Ruby Thomas asked. 'Is he young and handsome?' asked Josephine. 'Is he unmarried?' Jessie Milligan wanted to know.

'He's called Robert Grant, he's in his twenties, but I cannot tell you if he is handsome 'cos I've not seen a picture of him and I didn't think the Chairman would like that question,' Maggie twinkled at them. 'He will be with us for one year and then he goes back to the London office.'

'Go to it, Elsie,' her friends told her, 'this is your big chance.'

81

When Elsie-Nora told her mother, Mrs Ronby's happiness knew no bounds. Her imagination immediately took wing and did not rest until it saw Elsie-Nora as Mrs Robert Grant in Sussex (her preferred county) with her pukka English husband by her side in some stately mansion where she dispensed tea (a favourite vision) to friends and family. 'This is your chance, my girl,' she said, 'perhaps the last chance y'all will have. It's like an answer to my prayers. God is good, m'n, he's giving you a chance and remember, God helps those who help themselves. Y'all have to get out of here an' the only way to do that is to marry well and get out. Y'all have the looks and that's half the battle I tell you.'

'Oh, Mater,' protested Elsie-Nora, but it was a feeble protest because in her heart of hearts, she says, she knew it was what she wanted, just to get right away. After all, why not? Falling in love and India had not done anything for her.

'So,' said Mr Poddar with a sneer, 'it seems you are to be on loan to this chap Grant. I suppose you are very happy to have an Englishman as your boss? Just remember, you are only on loan and I hope you will learn something from him that will be useful when you come back to me.' His heavy-lidded eyes that reminded her of some bird of prey stared at her and he licked his lips, a habit that Elsie-Nora found unnerving.

'I don't know what you mean, sir,' she said coldly.

'Gain a little experience of this and that, this and that,' he said and licked his lips again.

Robert Grant, when he arrived, turned out not to be particularly good-looking. He was of medium height with fairly nondescript features, the exception being a pair of strikingly blue eyes. All the girls in the office decided instantly that he was a charmer and it had to be said that he was unfailingly courteous to them all, had a ready smile and a pleasant greeting for each of them and he never failed to say thank you for any service rendered. His 'English accent', the girls decided 'was just too cute for words.'

Robert may have seemed to Constantia Ronby the answer to a mother's prayers but he was, in fact, just one of the many Europeans who had started going then to India, as part of the technical cooperation many developing countries entered into to turn themselves from colonial dependencies into industrial nations.

The aid agencies too, began to move in around this time with what some were later to call the New Colonialism and ever more tourists swarmed to India with bigger and better planes to bring them in. Indian servants, more die-hard than any sahib, who had despaired when India became independent and the sahibs went, now found new openings for their roly-polys, rumble-tumbles, 'crum' cutliss', roast beef, even though the beef was more likely to be buffalo in deference to Hindu sentiment.

The dark and gloomy dining-rooms of the old hotels and Circuit Houses continued to serve spotted duck, caramel custard and Brown Windsor Soup, unaware that the new wave of foreigners were of a rather different breed, anxious to come to terms, or so they imagined, with the 'real India' and no sooner did they do so, than the strictures came too, thick and fast: India is dirty, it's full of beggars, if it isn't nailed to the ground 'they' will steal it.

And still they kept on coming, most notably the British, anxious to rediscover what had once been theirs and to describe the rediscovery countless times in the sort of articles that appear with regularity in the Sunday magazines. They came also to seek the mysticism and spirituality that was now commonly believed to be readily available in India and a new race of Indian 'godmen' was created, the antithesis of the western missionary, who had said 'thou shalt not' to the natives more often than not; these new gurus offered love, (usually sexual), and freedom from guilt to anxious, guilt-ridden young people from the west. They set up flamboyant empires across England and America where young white people dressed in Indian garb, heads shaven, danced and chanted 'Hare Krishna' while the statues of austere bygone statesmen looked down upon them with what could only be disapprobation.

'For Mater, this reappearance of Europeans was a welcome sight. Like the Indian government, but for different reasons, Mater was not well-disposed to English missionaries, who were among the few Britishers who stayed on after 1947. She used to say they ate only *dol** and rice like a Native and living so poorly. Sometimes I used to tease her and say if Jesus Christ appeared before her she would reject him an' all because he ate with his fingers and was not the fair-bearded, blue-eyed gent she imagined him to be!'

'Miss Ronby,' Robert Grant said, when she presented herself before him in the office that had been assigned to him, 'may I call you Elsie?' It was by way of being a rhetorical question as he had no intention of negotiating a mouthful like her ridiculous name every time he had to address her.

'Yes, of course, Mr Grant,' she answered demurely and thought that he did indeed have beautiful blue eyes.

'Good, thank you. Now, Elsie, you probably know that I shall be here for only one year, so there are a lot of things I will need to learn very quickly and I shall rely on you to put me straight whenever I need it. I assume you speak Hindi?'

Elsie-Nora blushed. 'Not too well, I'm afraid, sir.' What she meant was that she could give orders in Hindustani, her vocabulary consisting mainly of imperatives such as are used in speaking to the lower orders; words like *'ek dum'*, at once, *'hut jao'*, get out of the way, or simply *'jao'*, go.

Robert Grant looked surprised: 'Oh? Which is your language then?' He had been told that India had 14 official languages and several times that number of dialects.

'English,' replied Elsie-Nora and blushed again, 'I'm an Anglo-Indian, you see, sir.' She felt mildly vexed, as she was to be again many times in her later life, when those who should have known, seemed to know nothing.

Grant merely looked more bemused: 'Does that mean one of your parents is English?'

---

* This is how the Anglo-Indians pronounced it. The original word is 'dal'.

'Both my parents are Anglo-Indians, sir, but we have English ancestors.'

'I see,' said Robert, but did not look as if he saw at all, 'Yes, well, ah, I suppose you do know India and so you can help me there.'

'Yes, of course, sir,' Elsie-Nora mumbled and hoped that he would not too quickly discover her ignorance. She wished now she had paid more attention to the spoutings at the Tuesday Club; she was not at all sure that she knew even the names of all the Indian states. It had been easy when they were grouped into Presidencies, but now each one had an unpronounceable tongue-twister of a name.

Grant noticed her worried expression and he smiled kindly. 'Dinesh Poddar seemed sorry to lose your services, even temporarily, and the Chairman did say I was getting one of the best secretaries, so I'm certain we'll get on famously.'

And they did. RG, as he came to be called, was a considerate boss and as he was hard-working and conscientious himself, it never seemed a hardship to do a little extra for him.

The more Elsie-Nora saw of him, the more she liked him as a person. When, therefore, one day, when they had worked rather later than usual and RG suggested as he packed up his papers that they go out for dinner, Elsie-Nora agreed.

'It's a pity Shahpur doesn't have anything like a pub where one can grab a beer and a snack,' he said, 'Can you suggest somewhere nice?'

Elsie-Nora hesitated for a moment and then said: 'There's the Kwality restaurant. The food is good, it's clean and you could get a beer there, today is not a dry day.'

RG groaned comically, 'Oh, these dry days, they'll be the death of me. It always seems to be a dry day just when I'm hot and tired and panting for a cold beer.'

It was the first time Elsie-Nora had been back to the restaurant since Tarun had gone and she felt a pang which made her resist the waiter's attempts to seat her at the table they had always had.

'I don't know about you, Elsie, but I am starving. I could eat a horse,' said RG, after he had taken an appreciative gulp of ice-cold beer and he proceeded to order what seemed a vast amount of food. 'Yes, yes,' he said to the waiter, 'let's have it all, *rotis*, rice, curry and plenty of yoghurt to put out the fires,' he added.

The waiter was puzzled by the last word, 'Sir?' '*Dahi lao*,' Elsie-Nora translated.

'Yes sir, very good, sir,' the waiter grinned and vanished.

RG leaned back in his chair and looked at her. 'Now you must tell me something about yourself. We have been working together about two months and I know nothing about you.'

'Yes, you do,' Elsie-Nora countered, 'you know that I am an Anglo-Indian, that I can type and take shorthand and operate the cyclostyle.'

He laughed. 'And very well, too, I've got a very good secretary, but that is not what I meant and you know it.'

'What can I tell you? I've led a very boring life, never even been out of India.'

'What about your family? Let's start there,' he prompted.

'My father works on the railway and my mother is the matron at the Lady Curzon ... sorry, I mean the Kasturba Gandhi Hospital. It's been renamed, like everything else. I have two sisters; one is married to an Englishman and lives in Dorset and the other is married to another railwayman and lives here in Shahpur.'

'And you? No boyfriends, no marriage in the offing?'

'No,' Elsie-Nora blushed, because it was Robert whom she intended to marry before he returned to London, 'boyfriends, of course, but nothing serious.'

There was a pause as the waiter returned, laden with fragrantly steaming dishes, which he set before them. When they had served themselves and assuaged some of their hunger, Elsie-Nora said to RG: 'What about you, Mr Grant, have you a girlfriend back Home?'

'Oh, Robert, please, outside the office it's RG or Robert, whichever you prefer. Yes, I do have a girlfriend back in England. She's a doctor and takes her career very seriously. She's a lovely person is Sylvia.'

Elsie-Nora's heart had sunk when he had said he had a girlfriend, but as he continued she knew somehow that he was not in love with the lovely Sylvia. She sensed that it was one of those lukewarm relationships that would probably never ripen into anything more passionate, although she realized that it could end in marriage. Unless she did something about it and she was determined that she would; she recognized that this would probably be her last chance, as her mother kept telling her, and it was up to her to do something about it. She looked at him with what Kevin and Keith used to call her bedroom eyes, only to find that he was absorbed in the intricacies of using a *roti* as a scoop for his meat curry.

As Elsie-Nora lowered her eyes to her plate, she decided that she was going to do it. 'I liked him, it didn't seem to matter that I did not love him. I was going to go Home as RG's wife and I was going to spit in everyone's face, starting with that creep Poddar. Everyone was doing it, going to England for jobs, to study, there was always a long line to be seen in front of the Consular office of the British High Commission.'

It was a curious situation that Elsie-Nora found herself in. With Tarun's betrayal and departure, Elsie-Nora had given up on trying to be Indian. 'I just didn't want to know,' she says, 'and then there comes RG, one of those Englishmen who wants to know the real India, wants to immerse himself in it. He was one of those who thought that this would in some way make up for their insensitive imperialist forefathers. I wanted to tell him that all the old English rulers had not been mere plunderers only, they learned the languages, unearthed buried civilizations, translated literature, but he did not want to know. He was set on his quest for this real India of his and God help us, wanted me to help him!'

It was unfortunate that in this quest, poor RG was laid low by his encounter with Indian food. His very English constitution had only very briefly encountered Indian food in the Indian restaurants that were beginning to be set up in England and this bore little resemblance to the real thing served up in Shahpur.

'It doesn't taste at all like Indian food,' cried a disappointed RG.

However, this in no way diminished the search for knowledge and he drove Elsie-Nora almost to distraction with his constant questions, to most of which she rarely had satisfactory answers.

'Who cares, m'n, just make it up as you go along,' her mother advised. Brought up by her mother and the nuns at the convent to treat Hindu festivals as 'mumbo-jumbo' or 'heathen rituals', she could not distinguish among the many gods and goddesses of the Hindu pantheon and was unfamiliar with the customs and beliefs of Hindu India. She was well aware that RG was often puzzled by her.

Robert Grant, however, was becoming increasingly attracted to his secretary, although her accent and rather dated western clothes jarred upon him. It had soon become apparent to him that others in the office such as Dinesh Poddar, lusted after Elsie. Poddar had that tendency that some men think manly, to dig Robert in the ribs and make lewd remarks about having loaned him the services of his beautiful secretary.

Robert had never had much of a physical relationship with women. He had studied at all male institutions and had grown up before the sixties when, if one is to believe all that one reads, everyone decided to do their own thing and this usually meant plenty of sex with plenty of partners. Anything goes, they whooped, as they lived it up and along came AIDS and now we're all back to square one with monogamy coming back as the new buzz word instead of another word for boring.

To get back to Robert, his girlfriend Sylvia did not believe in sex without marriage and so she only allowed what in her own mind she probably termed 'liberties'. She and Robert were essentially just good friends who went on cycling trips or camping together, 'went dutch' at restaurants and shared a beer at their local.

RG was, therefore, very aware of good-looking Elsie-Nora who seemed to exude sensuality, all the men in the office were and they were inclined to be ribald about her and one or two of the other good-looking secretaries, with whom they liked to hint that they had had a 'good time'. RG assumed that by this euphemism they meant sex.

What puzzled Robert was that Elsie insisted on calling herself 'Anglo-Indian', wore only European clothes and seemed such an outsider, almost a foreigner like himself, in India. To him, she did not look English at all and he thought she would look like an Indian goddess in a sari, and on one occasion as he watched her enter his office dressed as usual in her tight short skirt and blouse, told her so. She smiled, rather grimly he thought, and shook her head: 'Not me, sir,' she said briefly and took up her dictation notebook, her pencil poised, indicating that she did not wish to discuss it.

RG found Indian women very attractive, but he did not find them friendly. The womenfolk of his colleagues were all sequestered away, appearing only on well-chaperoned occasions, definitely not available to go out with him alone. He was lonely, missing the familiar London scene, finding Shahpur somewhat claustrophobic and he missed the easy relationship and camaraderie he had with Sylvia. It was natural, therefore, that he turned to Elsie-Nora for feminine companionship and he began to take her out quite regularly despite, or perhaps because of, the inuendoes and envious looks that this occasioned among his colleagues.

Usually, they went out to dinner when it happened, as it did quite often, that they had worked late, causing Poddar and others to dig Robert in the ribs and make jokes about working overtime. They also went to the cinema when an English film was showing, though more often that not, it was some ancient film that Robert had already seen. This was followed by tea in Shahpur's only western hotel, the Cecil, a hangover from colonial days. They sat in the Palm Court restaurant where an Anglo-Indian pianist played a wistful, ragged sort of music, gypsy tunes, Hawaiian melodies, a muted and sentimental kind of jazz. The only palm, which presumably gave the restaurant its name, stood dustily in a green tub, looking very sorry for itself. 'I think,' said Robert, 'that they really mean the palms of quite another kind that appear on one's departure and into which small coins disappear with such miraculous rapidity.'

Sometimes, more infrequently, they went to the Shahpur Club. Robert found it depressing with its run-down air of a grande dame who has seen better days and all Elsie-Nora's attempts to make him understand what an important and wonderful place it had been in British times failed because RG could only feel guilt at what was to him an embarrassing anachronism. Now there were few if any foreigners to be found there, just the occasional visiting expatriate like himself and he found it pathetic and annoying the way the old bearers fell over themselves trying to serve him, as if the sight of a white skin had galvanized them. Even the Indians, now freely admitted where once they could never enter, seemed to prefer the bright new restaurants in town which had piped music, colour and noise.

'RG used to seem embarrassed by the whole thing,' Elsie-Nora remembered, 'He particularly disliked it when about three bearers tried to pull back his chair and to hover over him and he was embarrassed, he said, by the portraits of his bygone compatriots: the magistrates, district officers, colonels and all and he found himself trying to avoid their painted eyes which, he once said, seemed to follow him round the room. I used to find them fascinating and I never told him that in the not so very distant past I could not have entered there with him.' 'All of them all look haughty, isn't it?' she said to RG and he nodded: 'Awful,' he replied succinctly. But that was not what she had meant.

'Tarun never took me there and I thought it strange, but I suppose it wasn't really; obviously he was afraid we would run into someone he knew and then the fat would have been in the fire,' she said with a trace of lingering bitterness. 'Anyway, I had never been there before, never been a part of it and so I could not make him see its splendid past, its importance for the English people of those days, the heaven it was for them.'

'They say,' Elsie-Nora told RG, 'that sometimes at night, when it's all shut up, you can hear dance music and see people in evening dress when, in fact, there's no one there at all. Some of the servants swear they have heard carriages crunching up the gravelled drive,' she shivered and Robert laughed.

'They must be the bad sahib *log*,' he said, 'who couldn't get to heaven because this was their heaven. Or hell,' he added, as he looked at the club's ancient retainers, many more in number than the guests, waiting as if they expected that it would all happen once more, trying to ignore the children screaming round the once sacred snooker tables and flinging tomato sauce on the floor; trying to forget the dainty cucumber sandwiches and petits fours once served on silver plates, now routed by pakoras and chutney served on robust Gwalior pottery.

'The only survivor from the traditions of the past was the Gentlemen's Bar into whose recesses no lady could penetrate. I suppose Indian men being fond of their drink, found this British relic a useful refuge from nagging reproachful wives and so, in the name of tradition, it remained banned to women who sat in the lounge looking stoic.'

Chapter Seven

What RG did not know, and Elsie-Nora never attempted to enlighten him, was that these occasions when Elsie-Nora went out with her boss, threw her mother into a frenzy of delight. 'At last the girl is doing something sensible,' she told her family, 'He will propose, just y'all wait and see,' she told her husband, Gloria and Mary, 'then we can all of us all go Home.'

Gloria, informed of the delights that awaited her younger sister, was inclined to weep for she knew that by no stretch of the imagination could she be included in her mother's plans.

'It just isn't fair,' she stormed, 'first Ginny and now Elsie. Y'all never did anything for me,' she accused her mother, somewhat unfairly, and Mrs Ronby diplomatically ceased to tell Gloria of the progress of Elsie-Nora's affair.

Gloria's husband, generally referred to as poor Billy by the family, had been laid off work for 'drunken dereliction of duty' and now sat around the house all day drinking himself into a stupor, bemoaning his sad fate and beating up Gloria (though it must be admitted that he got as good as he gave) when she protested. More often than not, Gloria joined him in drowning their troubles and then the sale of chutneys and pickles did not prosper and the older children got into trouble because their school fees were not paid, or their uniforms were not in good order.

'Y'all,' said Mrs Ronby firmly, 'have only yourself to blame. Y'all had the opportunity, my girl, but y'all let it slip. There were a lot more Englishmen around when y'all were young an' all, but fool around with Lavvy Wilkins's son was what y'all chose to do, so now you just shut your gob an' wish your sister luck.'

Billy's mother Lavinia remained Constantia Ronby's *bête noire*, an enmity that dated from their long-ago school days when Lavinia Wilkins, despite her dark skin, had managed to entice Constantia's boyfriend away.

Sometimes, however, as the days lengthened into weeks and Elsie-Nora failed to report any significant change in the relationship, her mother would become annoyed by what seemed unnecessary dilatoriness on Robert's part. 'What's he waiting for?' she wanted to know, 'Does he need God Almighty to come down and give him a push or what?'

As this was directly addressed to her husband, Mr Ronby replied mildly: 'These things take time, Connie, my dear.'

'Time!' Connie snorted, 'That's exactly what he doesn't have. Lordy Moses, he's only here for a year, not for bloody eternity.'

Sometimes, she decided that Elsie-Nora must be at fault and then she would scold her: 'What y'all doin' wrong, that's what I'd like to know. Y'all had no trouble getting that Bengali babu boy to propose an' all.' When, as usually happened, Elsie-Nora left the room without deigning to reply, Mrs Ronby would turn to her unfailing confidante Mary: 'I'm not sure that girl has enough get up and go. When I was a young girl we knew how to bring a fellow to the point an' all. Only Ginny takes after me.' This last was delivered with a meaningful look at Horatio Ronby, as usual ensconced behind his paper.

It was Mary's suggestion that Elsie-Nora should invite the boss home for dinner. She was inclined to look upon herself as a family member and had been with the Ronbys for as long as Elsie-Nora could remember. Unless the mistress of the house was in an unusually bad temper, Mary freely offered her opinions and advice.

'Let him,' she said, 'come here and see for hisself that Missy baba has nice good European home,' she pronounced it 'yew rope pane', giving the word three very distinct syllables. 'Ronby sahib, he tells all about railways, good old British days, I makes the first-class Angrezi *khana* like they eats at Home. Then maybe he will be knowing for sure that the Missy baba she bloody good catch for him.'

Although Mrs Ronby had been given no clear role in this scenario, it was evident that she was much taken with the idea.

'Yes, my girl, that's the ticket, y'all invite him back here for dinner. A pukka English dinner: roast and two veg, soup of course, and one of Mary's best puddings.' She turned back to that functionary who was beaming all over her face at the success of her idea, 'Y'all see you get a really good leg of mutton, Mary and no cheating, y'all hear me? And roast the potatoes properly or I'll skin y'all alive I promise.'

'I working all these many long years European master madams only, I am knowing too damn well how to cook first class Angrezi *khana*,' Mary replied with dignity.

Mrs Ronby responded to this by telling her to bugger off and fetch the tea and not talk back to her betters, causing Mary to indulge in what her mistress described as 'crocodile tears', moaning that she 'was all alones in the world, a poor widow womans.' Nobody paid the slightest heed as everyone knew that her husband had, in fact, run away with the ayah from next door.

Elsie-Nora looked and felt dubious. She glanced round the room and thought that it looked shabby; she knew only too well how unpredictable her mother could be and Pater sometimes looked positively pathetic, there was something surreptitious about his manner.

She rather thought that RG came from a good family background. He had been to Oxford and the Public School he had attended was, she knew, one of the better ones. He was very modest, but some of the things he let drop painted a picture of a well-to-do family, educated and cultured. 'I thought to myself that he had more in common with the Sens than with the Ronbys! But I couldn't tell Mater that,' Elsie-Nora said ruefully.

Mrs Ronby, however, was enamoured of the idea that Robert Grant should come to Number 10, Railway Lines for dinner and she badgered her daughter incessantly. 'What are y'all waiting for, m'n?' she queried impatiently, 'Kingdom come? Y'all sit there shilly-shallying an' he'll have buggered off Home an' y'all'l be left here high and dry an' then, I tell you now itself, don't come cryin' an' complaining to me, like that Gloria now. No one listens to me, although I tell them an' tell them and then I've got to listen to all the belly aching afterwards. The only one of y'all three that's any good is Ginny an' she didn't get where she is by hanging about, I can tell you that straight.'

Elsie-Nora, nevertheless, did not extend the invitation to dinner to RG. Every day, questioned by her mother, she made one excuse or another, always making it appear that Robert had some other pressing engagement to fulfil.

When a fortnight had passed in this fruitless fashion and once again, Constantia Ronby's questions elicited a negative response from her daughter, she said: 'It looks to me, my girl, as if y'all ashamed of your home or something. Your pater and I have mixed with bigger people than your precious Mr Grant, I can tell you. I've just today had a letter from your godmother Elinor Graham from London and she's full of the good old days when we were friends here in Shahpur. We were good enough for the Grahams and he was the District Commissioner an' all when he died. So y'all just put that in your pipe and smoke it.'

'Okay, okay, Mater, I give in,' laughed Elsie-Nora, 'I'll invite RG to dinner, I promise you. Now tell me, what does Aunt Elinor have to say?'

'She asks after y'all and says it would be nice if you got the chance to visit her in London. She sounds lonely to me, those children of hers have no time for her and she seems to be having trouble with her arthritis. If she were here I would know what to do for her.'

There was a crash of breaking glass in the kitchen and Mrs Ronby stormed out of the room to investigate. She returned soon enough dragging a wailing Mary in her wake. 'How many times have I said y'all are not to touch that big bowl? I knew it would shatter as soon as your clumsy fingers like bananas touched it. Talk about butter fingers! Well, I shall cut twelve rupees from your pay.'

'I not help it, it not my faults,' protested Mary, weeping copiously, something she was quite talented at, 'Gloria Missy, she want chutney made in that bowl. What I can do?'

'Shut your noise, you silly creature,' said her mistress, 'and listen to this carefully. Missy baba going to bring her boss home for dinner and I want a first-class dinner prepared or I really will give y'all something to cry about.'

Mary stopped crying instantly and began to smile. 'I have good ideas,' she announced importantly, 'I makes snake and kidley pie for Missy baba friend. I am knowing that all European mens they loves the snake and kidley pie made by Mary.'

The Ronbys looked at each other and had to smile; nothing would convince Mary that it was steak and not snake, kidney and not kidley. 'She was a proper Mrs Malaprop,' remembers Elsie-Nora with an affectionate smile, 'we were always coming across the word 'penis' in her market accounts, when what she had bought was plain old beans. We just gave up trying to correct her.'

Mrs Ronby, however, countermanded the pie despite Mary's reiterations about its seemingly magical power that could turn dilatory young Englishmen into husbands. 'Y'all just do as you're told and get that leg of mutton.' Mrs Ronby then turned back to her daughter, while Mary stuck out her lower lip in mutinous protest, 'When should Mary get the leg for, Elsie?'

'Well,' replied Elsie-Nora evasively, 'I'll let y'all know. I'll have to pick a suitable occasion.'

'Suitable, my foot!' Mrs Ronby exploded, 'Y'all have to push yourself forward, m'n, if y'all want to get on in life. Trouble is, I ve said it before, but I'll say it again an' all, y'all are like your pater, no gumption the pair of you.'

'I tells you,' said Mary, determined to have the last word, 'snake and kidley pie the best, Mary make the very best. Missy baba friend, he so much happy he taste my snake and kidley pie, for sure he marry Missy baba.'

Chapter Eight

Robert Grant was meanwhile, becoming increasingly interested in his attractive secretary but some instinct, dimly chivalrous but also because he cherished his privacy, led him not to discuss his interest with the other men in the office. One or two of them had tried in an oblique fashion to discover whether he had bedded her; Robert found this puzzling because he had quickly learned that the code for women in India was strongly against sex before or outside marriage, the *Kamasutra* and erotic sculptures notwithstanding. Why then, he wondered, did they all seem to think Elsie-Nora would jump into bed with him?

Robert liked Elsie-Nora very much; she was not only very good-looking, she was also extremely good company. She was not serious or introverted like Sylvia and the few girls he had known while at University.

He was seeing a lot of her both at work and afterwards and enjoyed his evenings out with her so much that he was beginning to wonder if he was not falling in love. Robert was not sure that this would be a good thing, although he probably could not have explained why.

Unbidden, there came into his mind something that his grandmother had once said to him: 'Transplanted flowers take a great deal of tending, they do not flourish easily in unfamiliar soil.' As a young boy on vacation, he had been helping her to bed out seedlings taken from her hothouse into her garden in Lincolnshire and he had taken the remark as part of her gardening lore, but now the words came back to him as a warning. There was so much about Elsie-Nora Ronby that he neither knew nor understood.

When she invited him to come home and have dinner with her family, Robert hesitated. Was he, perhaps, getting in deeper than he wanted to go? Would Elsie see this as some form of commitment on his part? Then he felt ashamed of himself, it seemed so immodest to imagine that she was being anything other than friendly. Also, he had to admit, he was curious about her family and although curiosity was known to have killed the cat, in his case it won over prudence and Robert accepted the invitation.

On the evening, Robert went out and bought a large bunch of flowers from Shahpur's only florist and then wondered quirkily as he carried it home, whether this made him look more like a suitor than a colleague coming to dinner. In the end, after much hesitation, he pulled the flowers out of their cellophane wrapping and told his servant, Ali, who had been watching him with what looked like a knowing grin, to put them in a vase in the living-room.

While he watched this operation, it occurred to Robert that he ought not to arrive at the Ronby house empty-handed. He went to his liquor cabinet and withdrew a bottle of Scotch whisky from its depths, one of his small reserve of foreign whisky, and decided that this could safely be presented to Mr Ronby.

While he hesitated over the bottles, Robert noticed that Ali was in a state of suspended animation, a rose in his right hand poised for immersion in the vase, while he watched his master with deep interest. Although professing to be a devout Muslim who eschewed strong drink, Ali had been found making serious depredations into Robert's drink cabinet, resulting in Robert locking it up. What Robert did not know, but later suspected, was that Ali had in his possession a copy of every key in the house and that his employers never had any secrets from Ali.

As he drove to the Railway Colony, once pristinely Anglo-Indian, Robert noticed that it had a run-down look about it. Most of the houses were in need of a coat of paint and nearly all of them were festooned with washing; saris draped over balconies and along fences flowed down like vivid waterfalls and various undergarments and other clothes waved in promiscuous intimacy. Radios blared from most of the houses, providing a cacophony of Hindi film songs, classical music and recorded voices.

In some of the front gardens charpoys with rolls of bedding on them were placed where whole families squatted to enjoy the cool evening respite from the burning heat. They would, Robert knew, sleep out there, waking early before the sun grew fierce, wandering about in their night clothes, drinking early morning tea, or noisily brushing their teeth. He had come to the conclusion that Indians in their ablutions are noisier than most, and many travellers relate with amusement the dawn chorus as noses, mouths, throats, are cleared and emptied in readiness for the day ahead.

When Robert parked his car outside the Ronby gate, he noticed that the house, like most of the others, was shabby, its exterior unpainted, showing clearly the depredations of the weather. The garden (and RG loved gardens) was not well-tended, with more weeds than flowers proliferating in the untidy flower-beds.

The front door opened with disconcerting suddenness, almost before his finger had touched the bell. 'Good evenin', sar. Welcome our house, sar,' said the apparition that manifested itself in the doorway. A beaming Mary whose teeth, like the glass 'diamonds' at her ears, gleamed against her coal-black skin, ushered him in to where the master of the house sat by his radio. Robert was surprised to find that she spoke in English (if you could call it that, he thought wryly) to her employers. 'Sar, sar,' she said, 'here is Grant sahib, sar, Missy baba friend, come for dinner, sar.'

Mr Ronby rose hastily to his feet and looking guiltily about him, pulled on his jacket, before advancing to shake his visitor's hand. 'Mr Grant, sir, weall are honoured to have you in our house, sir,' he said. Although probably only in his fifties, Ronby looked old and somewhat wizened, with washed out blue eyes. His clothes hung awkwardly on him, giving the impression that they had been acquired at a jumble sale rather than made to measure.

'Mr Ronby, I'm delighted to be here, good of you and your wife to ask me. Please do call me Robert. And,' he added, holding out the wrapped bottle he had brought, 'here is a little something from me.'

Mr Ronby ducked his head with pleasure and said: 'Very good, Robert, thank you kindly. What can we offer y'all to drink, old man, whisky-*pani*, whisky-soda, or would y'all maybe prefer gin?'

'A whisky and soda would be very nice, thank you,' responded Robert. Mr Ronby, meanwhile, had begun to unwrap the bottle Robert had brought and Robert noticed that his hands were shaking.

Mary, who had been hovering eagerly, now darted towards her master and retrieved the paper from him as he was looking somewhat helplessly round him. Then, her smile as broad as ever, she scuttled off, returning almost immediately with glasses and soda, while Mr Ronby reached into the depths of a cupboard and drew out a half bottle of Indian whisky.

'Rot gut,' thought Robert and then smiled with simulated pleasure as his host held up the bottle as if for him to admire. Although Mr Ronby smiled back somewhat abstractedly, what Robert did not know was that he was checking to see whether his son-in-law had been at the bottle.

While Mr Ronby carefully poured out two minute shots of whisky from a peg measure firmly affixed to the bottle, Robert looked around him. He suppressed a smile at the pictures of the British Royal Family (he had been told about a group that called itself Empire Loyalists, singing "God Save The King" and saluting the Union Jack) and his eye took in the embroidered texts, not missing the one that proclaimed that God and not his host was the head of the house.

He noticed the antimacassars on the chairs, the profusion of lace doilies on every surface. Rather dusty artificial flowers, among them some rather improbable looking blooms, stood in metal containers on low tables and on the radio which was covered with a lace cloth. Robert could not help wondering what would have happened to his flowers had he brought them.

There was nothing remotely Indian in or about that room and something about it teased at the corners of his memory, a vague sense of *déjà vu*. It was only when he rose to greet

Elsie-Nora and her mother that it came to him: he had once been in the home of his mother's daily and that was what he had been reminded of.

Mr Ronby, in the act of lifting his glass to clink it against Robert's, saying: 'Cheers, old man, bottoms up,' spun round as the women entered the room. He lifted his glass to Elsie-Nora and said with a wink: 'See, girly, your gentleman-friend and your old pater have made friends, isn't it Mr, er, I mean Robert?'

Elsie-Nora looked beautiful as she smiled affectionately at her father. 'Good for you, Pater, ' she said and then shook hands with Robert. 'Now I'd like you to meet my mother, RG,' she said.

Robert looked with interest at Mrs Ronby. There were, he saw, vestiges of Elsie-Nora's looks, but the mother was stout and her silk dress was too tight. She had powdered her face and neck rather too liberally, contriving to give herself a sort of puce-coloured complexion, her arms and shoulders contrasting rather strangely with her face. On her feet she wore something that looked like bedroom slippers.

All smiles, Mrs Ronby approached him and held out her hand for him to shake with a somewhat coy expression on her face. 'Oh, Mr Grant, isn't it? Elsie-Nora has told us so much about you, but I won't repeat it because we don't want your ears to burn an' all, do we? We feel we know y'all already, isn't it, Pater? We're so pleased to be able to entertain y'all in our house, be it ever so humble. It is a long time since we had anyone from Home visiting us.'

Robert, who through this speech had been left holding her hand like a tea tray, was puzzled by her last remark, but he greeted her warmly and thanked her for inviting him. He was beginning to perspire from mingled heat and embarrassment and wondered whether he would be permitted to remove his jacket. Since, however, he had seen his host don his on his arrival, Robert rather doubted it and tugging uncomfortably at his tie, he wished he had had the sense to wear a thinner shirt. He was not to know, but Mrs Ronby believed that it was not genteel to sit down to dinner in shirtsleeves when one had company. Elsie-Nora, therefore, had to ignore his mute appeal and Robert prepared to suffer.

Horatio Ronby displayed the bottle Robert had brought to his wife and daughter, then ducked his head again in acknowledgement, while Mrs Ronby bestowed upon him a regal smile. Robert looked deprecating. He noticed that the bottle, after this ritual introduction, disappeared from view and was locked away in the cupboard. Robert wondered whether the maid, like his bearer, was given to tippling?

Constantia Ronby was saying in a queenly fashion: 'It is very kind of y'all, but there was no need. My hubby,' this with a menacing glance at her hapless spouse, 'keeps quite enough to drink in this house.' She then seated herself on the sofa and patted the place beside her. There was no possible reply that Robert could think of, so he merely looked deprecating again and meekly sat down beside his hostess.

Mrs Ronby's mode of conversation was to introduce a subject, usually in the form of a question, sometimes as a statement, then after a suitable amount of time, to introduce another. When she came to the weather, Robert brightened and agreed emphatically that Shahpur was unbearably hot for the time of year. This did not have the desired effect, however, for instead of inviting him to divest himself of his jacket, she jumped and seized a palmetto fan and proceeded to fan herself and him with vigour, sometimes catching him on the side of his head with a resounding thwack. At each collision she made a clicking sound with her teeth and apologized, whereupon Robert smiled weakly and said 'not at all' and felt a fool.

'I come from Sussex myself,' Mrs Ronby informed him, 'Dy'all know it at all?' While he was trying to work out what she meant by this, the lady had moved on to Dorset: 'My eldest daughter lives there with her English husband. Thank goodness, Mr Grant, that she was able to get out of this wretched country before independence and was able to go Home where we all belong and that is where we all will go as soon as Elsie-Nora is settled.'

Robert did not know what she meant by Home and imagined that she was referring to their moving out of the Railway Colony into a house of their own.

'How do you mean settled?' he asked and then he realized what the answer would be and wished it unasked.

Constantia Ronby bestowed on him a smile of such devastating archness that poor Robert flinched: 'Why, married of course, to a nice Englishman. Then we'll all of us all go Home.'

Robert glanced across at Elsie-Nora and saw that she was blushing. 'Mater,' she said and the desperation in her voice was evident, 'shouldn't you tell Mary about dinner?'

'Don't interrupt, my girl, when I'm talking to our guest. We are having a nice chat, aren't we, Mr Grant?' she turned to him with a gracious smile and managed to clip him with the fan. 'Elsie is still only a little girl to her pater and me, but we know she will marry soon and she is a beautiful girl though I say it myself. She has had many chances and I tell her with her looks an' all, she can marry anyone. I'm sure y'all agree with me, isn't it?'

Elsie-Nora jumped up in an attempt to stem her mother's flow and Robert was spared the necessity of a reply for the door opened and a man and woman entered the room. Robert guessed that this must be Elsie's sister and her husband. The woman was a smaller, younger version of Mrs Ronby, also running to fat, dressed in a flashy red dress that had obviously been made for her in her younger, slimmer days; now it was held together in places by safety pins, its owner clearly being no needlewoman. For the rest of the evening those hard-working pins exercised a dreadful fascination for Robert who wondered how far they would go before being forced to give up the unequal task of holding the dress together round its occupant.

'I didn't know y'all were coming here tonight,' Robert heard Elsie-Nora say in a sibilant whisper. Gloria bridled: 'Any reason why not? We all not good enough for your posh boyfriend?'

'Oh, shut up, Gloria,' hissed Elsie-Nora *sotto voce*, as she thought.

'Y'all have a bloody nerve talking to me like that,' Gloria hissed back.

'My girls are devoted to each other and so they should be,' simpered Mrs Ronby, 'After all, who else do they have in the world after my hubby and I have passed on?' She rose with a creaking of joints and seized her elder daughter by the hand, pulling her towards the sofa from which Robert had politely risen. 'This, Mr Grant, is my middle girl Gloria-Jean,' she turned to where, like a tug following a liner, her son-in-law followed in her wake, 'and this is my son-in-law Bill, William Wilkins.'

There was something hangdog and pathetic about Bill. His eyes were bloodshot and having wrung Robert's hand in a moist handshake, he gazed with undisguised longing at Robert's glass which he had set down on a table. Robert realized at once that it was because of Bill and not the blameless Mary that the cupboard had been locked. During the evening he intercepted many a longing glance that the luckless Mr Wilkins cast in that direction. He noticed, too, that apart from an orange squash brought by Mary, no strong drink was offered to the son-in-law.

Elsie-Nora had remained standing by the door and she looked angry. Despite his own discomfort, Robert felt sorry for her and so he smiled and retrieving his glass from Bill's drooling attentions, he raised it to her. She smiled back, then with a shrug of her shoulders, she came back into the room. Taking the palmetto fan from her mother, she replaced it among the other bric-à-brac and neatly interposed herself on the sofa beside Robert before her mother could resume her seat. It was not enough, however, to deter Mrs Ronby who said: 'That's right, y'all two sit together and enjoy yourselves while I get Mary to dish up.' She bestowed on Robert a smile of encouragement.

There was silence after Constantia Ronby went out of the room. Mr Ronby seemed to huddle in his ill-fitting jacket, sitting on the edge of his chair as if poised for escape. Gloria stared fixedly at Robert and her husband's gaze never veered from

Robert's glass, watching its progress from the table to his lips and back.

'Seen any good pictures recently?' Gloria asked suddenly. She pronounced it 'pitchers'.

'Not recently, no. Most of those showing now are old ones I've seen already.'

'D'y'all like it here? What I mean to say is, don't y'all miss England. Home,' she added with a lingering wistfulness.

'Can't say that I do, not yet. I find it all fascinating here, I love India and I should imagine it's cold and rainy in England right now. Anyway, I'll be back there in a few short months.'

Gloria's eyes immediately shot to her sister's face, her interested scrutiny making it plain that she had not been informed that Robert was in India for only a short time. A coy smile, dreadfully reminiscent of her mother, came to her lips: 'And what, pray,' she said in an artificial voice, 'are y'all going to take back Home from here and all? I bet I can guess, no?' and she was clearly going on to say more, when Elsie-Nora rose abruptly from her seat beside Robert and trod heavily on her sister's toes encased in tight red high-heeled pumps.

'Ouch,' squealed the unfortunate Gloria, 'can't y'all see where y'all bloody going you great clumsy cow?' but the pain in her foot preoccupied her thoughts and diverted her from what she had been about to say.

At this somewhat fraught moment, the sisters glaring at each other like prizefighters before the next round, with Gloria massaging her toes, Mr Ronby looking longingly at his radio over which his wife had angrily twitched a lace cloth, Bill seized Robert's glass and drained it in one convulsive gulp and hiccuped gently just as Mrs Ronby came bustling back.

Constantia Ronby surveyed the scene grimly, then essayed a smile for Robert's benefit. 'D'y'all need to powder your nose?' she asked him. With her left hand she seized the empty glass out of Bill's hand, while with the other she motioned Robert to the bathroom. Feeling yet another rivulet of sweat run down his chest, Robert decided to take the opportunity of splashing himself with some cold water.

When he returned, Mary, grinning as broadly as ever, was waiting to escort him to the dining table where the Ronbys had already seated themselves, with Horatio Ronby at the head of the table, his napkin tucked into his shirt collar. There was the sort of silence that occurs when someone enters a room and everyone stops talking; it was clear that the family had been in the middle of a heated exchange.

Mary placed soup in front of everyone. In the middle of the table stood an array of sauces, tomato, Worcestershire and brown sauces. Just as Robert lifted his spoon, without any warning Mr Ronby launched into a lengthy Grace, in the course of which he thanked the Almighty for many things and for divinely vouchsafing to the Ronbys the opportunity for fellowship with Robert.

No sooner had he finished, almost before Amen had been intoned, Mrs Ronby leant forward: 'Mulligatawny soup, Mr Grant. Not an English soup, I know, but mistakes will happen,' this with a glare at Mary who rolled her eyes and muttered under her breath, 'However, this is Elsie-Nora's favourite soup and I hope you like it too.'

'It's very good,' said Robert and so it was, a pleasant blend of meat, spices, lime juice and rice. No sooner had he said so than Mary was at his side, soup-ladle at the ready, teeth and earrings glinting. 'No thank you, no more,' Robert smiled at her. 'It's really extremely good, but I can't have any more.'

Mr Ronby had seemed immersed in his soup, carefully spooning up the last drops, but now he looked up to say: 'Mulligatawny soup is what y'all might call a hybrid dish Mr ... er ... I mean Robert. It is an Anglo-Indian dish, Indian spices, but an English soup.'

'In Tamil it mean pepper-water,' put in Mary, soup-ladle still at the ready as if this bit of information might spur Robert into having more.

106

'Bugger off with the plates,' her mistress told her. Mrs Ronby sighed and said to Robert: 'It is so difficult to train these Natives properly, y'all have no idea.'

'Where is she a native of?' asked the naïve Robert. Gloria giggled, a high-pitched sound.

'She's Indian, of course,' Mrs Ronby was surprised.

'I wondered why she speaks to you in English?' ventured Robert, who had begun to perspire again from a combination of mulligatawny, with its peppery after-taste, and discomfort.

'Because we all are European, of course, we don't speak her native gibberish,' Mrs Ronby said, as if it was the most obvious thing in the world. Completely flummoxed and out of his depth, Robert decided that he must somehow have strayed like Alice into Wonderland and he waited for the White Rabbit or some other strange character to appear.

While Mary changed the plates, Robert glanced at Elsie-Nora but found that she avoided his eyes and so he glanced round the room instead. There was yet another embroidered text in this room, this one claiming that there was an invisible guest at the table. Robert recognized the *Monarch of the Glen*, a picture he had a fondness for, he remembered, when he was a child. He said so, earning a smile of approval from his hostess.

Rather dingy lace curtains hung at the windows and through them came the strains of a sitar. Mrs Ronby rose abruptly and banged the windows shut saying: 'Believe me, Mr Grant, things were not so when the English were here. Now we have Indian neighbours and must put up with the caterwauling they all call music, which they play loudly all day and night. They cook their smelly Indian food, but what to do? Weall just have to grin and bear it.'

'Actually I like Indian music, although I can't say I understand it and I must say I prefer the smell of Indian food to the smell of boiled cabbage.'

At that precise moment, Mary bore in the cabbage which was to accompany the roast mutton masquerading as lamb, lying like a wet rag in its dish and identified for Robert the smell of wet washing which had greeted him earlier, a smell that lingers in many an English hallway.

Robert's face turned brick-red, while three pairs of eyes looked at him with astonishment and dismay. Elsie-Nora looked away and Bill Wilkins alone remained unmoved, smiling vacuously to himself.

'Well, I never!' exclaimed Constantia Ronby, 'It's that sort of attitude that caused the end of the British Raj, y'know.'

'Surely it had to end some time,' Robert said feebly, wishing himself miles away. He was now sweating profusely.

Horatio Ronby looked up from carving the meat, which he cut into almost transparent slivers.

'Y'know, old man, things aren't the same here any more. Y'all take the railway, when our lot ran it, it was tiptop. Now it's not the same, the trains run late, the carriages an' all are filthy.'

'Indians just don't have our standards,' Mrs Ronby informed him firmly.

Everybody seemed to expect that he would make some kind of rejoinder and so, against his will, Robert said defensively: 'People have a right to be independent. They may make mistakes at first, but it's their country and they must be allowed to get on with it. And maybe they seem mistakes to us, but are all right in their own context.'

The Ronbys looked at each other and everyone seemed about to say something, but Gloria beat them to it: 'What about us lot then?' she asked truculently, 'Weall are not Indian, what are we all supposed to do then?'

Robert mopped his brow with his damp handkerchief and then realized that it was not a rhetorical question; the Ronbys were waiting for his reply. He glanced at Elsie-Nora but she averted her eyes. 'Perhaps,' he replied, 'you have to decide who you are and where you want to be.' He took a deep breath and added foolhardily: 'Perhaps you should forget about the Anglo, it all seems so far-away and unimportant, and rediscover the Indian.'

This time, says Elsie-Nora, he might as well have got up and flung a bomb in their midst. Mrs Ronby and Gloria were outraged and were silent only because they could hardly speak for rage. Mr Ronby seized the opportunity thus afforded and said: 'Well, young man, y'all certainly do have some funny ideas, no? We are Domiciled Europeans, you know, we cannot become Indian at the drop of a hat just because the English have gone away and left us lot in the lurch.' He shook his spoon at Robert, 'Y'all mark my words, Mr Grant sir, England won't be the same an' all without the Empire. Once y'all let the side down, lose the old values, the country will just go down the drain.' The others nodded in agreement.

Robert cleared his throat uncomfortably and ran his finger round his shirt-collar which seemed suddenly intent on choking him. The Ronbys all stared at him as if they expected him to capitulate. He was goaded into speech: 'Well, I'm sorry, but I don't agree. I think one has to come to terms with reality, not live in a world that has passed away. Britain's empire is finished and not before time. It's India for Indians now.'

Robert could not know, but these words of his, innocent though they seemed to him, reminded Horatio and Constantia of their old foe, Nikhil Sen. It had been his battle cry at the height of the Quit India movement: 'India for Indians only, British and their mongrels out.'

'Well, I never,' Mr Ronby seemed to swell with emotion, 'we all never expected to be stabbed by our own side an' all.'

His wife was more explicit: 'I suppose y'all'l be saying next y'all want Elsie-Nora to dress up in a sari and behave like a Native with all their nasty dirty habits.'

Robert looked at Elsie-Nora and this time she met his eyes. She looked at him in mute appeal. 'That is her business,' he answered levelly, 'what she wants to wear or how she behaves, but I am certain that she will continue to look lovely whatever she wears.'

Although mollified somewhat, Constantia Ronby was not appeased, but the atmosphere lightened somewhat and she reassumed her earlier gracious smile, even if its cordiality was somewhat dimmed. 'She is a beautiful girl, and we think she can marry anyone she wants, no?'

It was Gloria's turn to scowl. 'Looks aren't everything. Y'all always say, Mater, catch your hare before y'all can cook it,' this with a malicious look at her sister. Robert was becoming desperate again. He pushed away his plate and said formally: 'I am sure that whoever has the good fortune to marry Elsie will be a very lucky man indeed.' Elsie-Nora knew that he was saying that it would not be he.

The cabinet pudding had been eaten, the coffee drunk; they rose at last from the table and release was in sight for both Elsie-Nora and Robert.

Chapter Nine

To Elsie-Nora the evening had seemed interminable. She knew it had gone wrong almost from the beginning with her family showing itself in its worst light. She shuddered when she thought of how the evening had turned out. She had known somehow that it was doomed when Gloria had walked through the door dressed in that dreadful red dress followed by Billy slavering over poor RG's drink.

Mater had been herself, only more so, trying to impress on Robert how British a family was theirs, while poor old Pater had looked more than usually ineffective, as if in some way diminished by Robert's presence. Elsie-Nora wished passionately for the hundredth time that she had never consented to her mother's and Mary's plan. 'I saw the way RG looked at us all and at our house and I knew that at best he pitied me and at worst he despised us all.'

It had been made clear to Robert that the Ronbys looked on him as Elsie-Nora's boyfriend, the one who would help her to escape from India, help them all escape Home to England where they thought they belonged. Such a prospect might not seem dire to a man deeply in love, but to a clear-headed Robert the thought of returning to London with the entire Ronby clan in tow, Gloria, safety pins and all, was unthinkable. Being in love, really head over heels·in love, might have helped to sweeten the pill that was Constantia Ronby; after all, we are told by poets and philosophers that love is blind and even, at times, mentally retarded. Robert was, alas, in full possession of his senses and he realized that Elsie-Nora was not for him.

From Elsie-Nora's point of view the evening was an unmitigated disaster and the very next day at the office, although RG thanked her very politely for the 'interesting evening with her family', she sensed a difference in his behaviour. He was cooler, more distant, as if he was withdrawing from her, denying that there had been the beginnings of something deeper. Elsie-Nora understood then why her sister Ginny had never

111

brought John Wells home to Shahpur to meet her family, preferring to slip away quietly with him to England.

'I always did say I was born both too early and too late. The English in India after independence now wanted "Indianness", the very thing that had been held at arms length and held in suspicion since the Mutiny, a quality of foreignness and exoticism. As Elsie-Nora Ronby, I did not fill that bill. You see, India was being kind of rediscovered by the Brits, no longer a colony, but the fountainhead of wisdom, yoga, mystery; what was once thought bizarre and even sinister was now being openly sought. Our Ronby brand of Britishness was unexciting, not full of eastern promise,' Elsie-Nora smiled a little sadly, 'something they were now ashamed of.'

Robert might have changed in his attitude to Elsie-Nora, but he was still very powerfully attracted to her and he still liked her. Robert desired Elsie-Nora but was too cautious to make any advances and he also had no desire to hurt her. He had understood that the goal was matrimony and that he was not prepared to offer. So the invitations to the Palm Court and to the Club ceased and Robert's behaviour towards her was now irreproachably correct.

It is hard to say how things might have turned out had everyone left well alone. Perhaps Robert would have been drawn back to Elsie-Nora, might have been made to understand that he did not have to shoulder the entire Ronby family, and given their propinquity and her undeniable charm, they might have had a conventional happy ending. Or one might speculate that had Elsie-Nora not gone with Robert to Poddar's party, she might have ended up differently. Who can tell? There is always cause and effect, but not always clearly apparent.

Poddar decided to throw a party. 'You will soon be gone from here,' he was heard telling RG, 'It's time we had a really good bash at my place, a sort of office party. Good for company morale and all that,' he winked at Robert and slapped him on the back. 'No doubt you will bring Miss Ronby,' he said and leered.

Elsie-Nora, disliking Poddar as she did, was inclined to refuse his invitation. Her mother thought otherwise. She had been in a thoroughly bad humour after Robert had left her house, angry with everyone for the way they had behaved and not at all pleased with Robert himself. 'Just the sort of young Britisher who's too wet behind the ears to know anything, but who thinks he knows it all,' she remarked.

'Be that as it may,' opined Constantia Ronby, 'y'all'l be a fool not to attend the party. While there's life there's hope and y'all shouldn't give up so easily. Mr Grant thinks y'all beautiful and we could see he fancies y'all all right. In any case, if y'all don't play your cards right, that Poddar will continue to be your boss after Mr Grant leaves and y'all better not forget that, my girl.'

Against her better judgement, Elsie-Nora went to the party with Robert. He came to the Railway Colony to pick her up but stayed in his car at the gate, tooting his horn to alert her to his arrival. The lace curtains at the window twitched and he thought he could see the flash of Mary's teeth; curtains on both sides of the Ronby house were opened and the Ronby's offending Indian neighbours looked out at him with open interest.

Elsie-Nora wore again the black lace dress she had worn so many moons ago to the Sen party. 'You look very lovely, Elsie,' Robert said as she got into his car, 'really very beautiful.'

'I'm glad you think so, sir,' she said demurely.

'Come on now, you know it's RG or Robert after office hours and this is definitely after office hours.'

'That,' says Elsie-Nora, 'was very apparent when we arrived at the party. The other executives had also brought along their secretaries and by the time we got there most of them had drunk quite a bit and everyone was flirting outrageously. There was no sign of Poddar's wife and he apologized for her absence, saying she was shy and didn't speak much English. Hah!'

Robert got them both a drink and then turned away to greet someone. Elsie-Nora stood alone for a moment, thoughtfully sipping her drink and looking round her.

'Well, fancy meeting you again,' said a vaguely familiar voice behind her and Elsie-Nora turned to find Tarla's friend standing beside her. She groped in her memory for his name and remembered that Tarun had called him Jagdish *dada*. For a moment she felt sick as old memories washed over her, almost a sense of *déjà vu*, as she remembered that other fateful party where she had met Tarun.

Dr Bannerji was saying in that soft Bengali voice of his that Elsie-Nora had come to hate: 'You are ... Miss er ... you are Tarla's friend, aren't you?'

The sight of his face so near her own, his round thick-lensed glasses behind which his eyes still swam like frisky fish, caused Elsie-Nora's face to tighten, her expression cold. 'My name is Miss Ronby. A long time ago, yes, I was Tarla's friend and then we both grew up.'

'Still as beautiful as ever,' said he, oblivious of her coldness.

Robert rejoined her and Dr Bannerji's fish eyes became quite frantic. 'Well, well, RG, you lucky chap, you with this lovely lady?' He smiled and Elsie-Nora did not care very much for that either.

'You two know each other?' she asked.

'We knew each other slightly at University, lived on the same staircase for a year, and then we met again here the other day,' Robert explained. Bannerji put his arm around RG's shoulders and drew him away saying: 'I must tell you what I heard the other day about John Latimer, would you believe . . . .'

RG threw an apologetic look at Elsie-Nora over his shoulder and murmured: 'Back in a moment, Elsie, wait for me.'

Elsie-Nora stood there and watched them go off together towards the bar. They were met there by Poddar and one or two of the other men and there was much back-slapping and poking in the ribs accompanied by guffaws.

Obviously, since Elsie-Nora did not hear what the men said to each other that evening, I have had to rely on my inventive powers to piece together what she thinks they might have said, but I do believe that what follows is not far from the truth and Elsie-Nora agrees with me.

'You have caught everything but their smirks, winks and nudges, the dirty bastards,' she says without heat, for her anger has long been tamped down and nothing remains but the memory of it.

'Well, old chap, have you scored with her yet?' asked Bannerji as soon as they had moved out of earshot, 'You know, I wouldn't mind having a go myself, but she doesn't fancy the likes of me, I have nothing to offer her.'

'How do you mean?' asked Robert, avoiding an answer to the question.

'My dear chap, I mean she's a gold-digger like all her tribe. In the old days they were all after any Englishman they could get, but this one of yours was clever enough to try and entangle my fiancée's brother who was young and stupid. Marriage to Tarun Sen would have been a real coup for her, but you know Nikhil Sen, he soon got rid of her and without giving her so much as a penny. Now I expect you've come along like manna from heaven; better make sure she doesn't entangle you in her net in order to get out of here and Go Home where they fondly imagine they belong.'

'On the other hand,' put in Poddar who had joined them, 'if you dangle that bait before her, she'll probably do anything for you,' he laughed and shoved Robert in the ribs. 'She's hot stuff,' he went on, licking his lips, 'take my word for it,'

The others turned to him: 'Do you mean you...?'

Poddar smirked. 'That would be telling,' and he laid a finger against his nose. 'But I'll tell you this, RG, old chap, you should have no problem. They are all good-time girls, and you've taken her out often enough.'

Dr Bannerji looked reflective: 'Maybe it's the mixed blood, but these girls have no morals, alley cats all of them, I suppose it must be because they are the product of the worst of both our races.'

Into Robert's mind came a vision of Mrs Ronby who said she was from Sussex and the claustrophobic quality of that little bungalow in the Railway Colony. There had been an aura of respectability about it all, the embroidered texts, the roast and two veg and yet, they had flung Elsie-Nora at him all evening. Had they thought they could so easily entrap him?

Jagdish Bannerji nudged him and winked: 'Have a good time, old man, but don't get landed with her. Anglos are for fun, not for marrying.'

To clinch matters, Poddar, who had imbibed far more than was good for him, leaned forward at a perilous angle and said: 'You see that girl our Miss Ronby is talking to? Ruby Thomas? I've had her any number of times and you cannot imagine the sexual tricks that girl knows. All I have to do to keep her sweet is to make sure she gets a regular increment.' He laughed, preened himself and nearly fell over, saving himself by placing his hand on Robert's shoulder. 'You've got to know how to handle these girls, then you can have all the fun you want.'

Elsie-Nora says that RG had too much cheap Indian whisky that night, she says it as if in extenuation. 'He wasn't himself. He became angry with himself, as if somehow he had been tricked out of something by his own stupidity. I suppose those other men made him feel he had missed out on something that was there for the taking and there was something unmanly about his failing to have done so.'

When RG danced with her she knew that he was not himself. He held her in a tight embrace and his hands were rough as they strayed over her breasts and buttocks. The lights in the room had been dimmed and this, too, gave him a courage he might not otherwise have possessed.

He whispered words into her ears, but they were not endearments. 'What a lovely bitch you are, Elsie,' he said, 'just like a bitch in heat, all these men after you like randy dogs. But you are going to come home with me tonight, aren't you, my little beautiful bitch? You are going to give me a good time for a change.'

Elsie-Nora does not try to explain why she did what she did that night. I do not think she cared very much one way or another and she did not place much importance on the whole business of sex, treating it as something one did if one was in the mood and could be sure one was safe from unwanted pregnancy.

She knew, she had always known, that Robert wanted to sleep with her. She had not let it come to anything because it had been her trump card. In those days, it often was; many people got married out of sheer sexual frustration. That evening, however, she knew he had been primed by the other men and the alcohol. She had seen them leering at her and it had not been difficult to guess what was being said because all her life she had grown up with the knowledge that Indian men talked like that about girls like her, as loose women and therefore, as fair game.

Well, she was going to do as they expected, she was going to sleep with RG because she liked him and he wanted her and to hell with everybody and everything! She had resigned herself to losing Robert, now she would give him a souvenir and send him on his way.

When she got into his car to go home he turned at once to her and began kissing her. She could smell the whisky on his breath and caught a faint whiff of his aftershave. Robert's hand found its way to her breast, while his other hand went lower, seeking her innermost recesses. That was the moment, she says, when she hesitated and wondered whether, in fact, all was lost. If she slept with him, might he come to realize that he loved her, cared for her enough to take her away with him?

'I want you, Elsie,' he murmured, his hand fumbling with her buttons, his mouth moving to encircle her nipple on which he sucked hard, like a little baby. Then he raised his head and looked at her: 'You know I have always wanted you, will you come home with me tonight?' He did not mention love, he was honest enough to make no pretences and if she had refused, Elsie-Nora thinks he would have driven her home.

'Why not?' she replied and wondered why she had said that; quickly, she added: 'Yes, Robert, if that is what you want.' She felt cold and detached and when they went to his house she responded automatically to his hands and his mouth, said and did the right things, writhing against him, raking his back with her nails, while all the time in her mind she reviewed the possible outcome.

Many of us women have, or think they have, little but our bodies to offer and so it is only natural that we put a high price on this, our beauty, expecting to barter it for love, security, happiness, even a career. How many times have we all said when a man is seen with a plain woman: 'Wonder what he sees in her', as if without attractiveness, a woman should be invisible to a man. On the other hand, in Elsie-Nora's case, it might also have been that she valued her body so little that she saw no harm in offering it in exchange for a possible passage to England. I asked her this and she smiled her beautiful smile. 'Y'all are too clever for me, my girl, I haven't the faintest what y'all mean.'

Elsie-Nora slept with Robert a great many more times before he left Shahpur and he did begin to love her after a fashion. Elsie-Nora's ready acquiescence, however, only confirmed in his mind the truth of what Poddar and the others had said. People in those days thought like that in England; 'nice girls' didn't and girls themselves believed that if they 'gave themselves' (dreadful phrase) to their lovers before marriage the men would lose interest, having got what they wanted (another dreadful phrase), or if you prefer, after they had had their wicked way!

Since Robert did not want to marry Elsie-Nora, he wanted to believe that she was just a good-time girl with whom any man might have a little fun before going on his way. I think he knew better; that is why he bought her all those expensive presents and why sometimes, as on the last occasion they were together, he broke down and wept and asked her to forgive him for the way he had treated her. That was when he told Elsie-Nora about his grandmother and her advice about transplanted flowers. Later, ashamed of his outbursts, he asked her to forgive those as well, ascribing them to too much Indian whisky which, together with a number of other Indian things, he found did not suit him at all.

Chapter Ten

It was time for Robert Grant to return home to England and he knew it was time that he went. On his last night with Elsie-Nora he broke down completely and asked her to forgive him and she says she sensed in him a deep sadness at the way things had turned out. I think she would like to believe that he loved her and was sad about the way it had gone wrong; but then Elsie-Nora loves those soppy old movies where she can have what she calls a 'good cry'. But then again, she may be right or, being an essentially decent young man, Robert felt guilty about the way he had treated her, knowing as he must have, that right to the end she had hoped he would care enough to take her with him. Paradoxically, being a woman, it was herself she blamed for her failure and of course, her mother did not hesitate to rub it in by telling her she had not played her cards right.

Good-natured, happy-go-lucky Elsie-Nora had played the cards she had, those which character, upbringing and circumstance had put into her hand, how should she be expected to play them any other way? We cannot play another's hand, only our own, and Elsie-Nora played the hand she had been dealt and lost that particular game. She knew she had lost, but she went on playing until Robert's last day and then she knew she must get away, must engineer her escape from that leering Poddar and the other men, even from the other girls in the office, get right away from Shahpur with all its associations and its inevitable limitations.

Standing at the bus-stop that morning, Elsie-Nora had been accosted by a young woman, little more than a girl really, although she held an infant in her arms and another child clung to her sari. She asked Elsie-Nora if the number nine bus would take her to Nawabgarh. Assured that it would she looked shyly but admiringly at Elsie-Nora and hesitantly enquired how many children the memsahib had. 'None,' replied Elsie-Nora shortly, 'I am not married.'

The girl's eyes grew round. 'Not married and so beautiful? Memsahib's mother must be getting worried.'

120

You could say that, thought Elsie-Nora grimly, aloud she said in her halting Hindi: 'I am a working woman.' The girl looked impressed and confided that she had been married young to a man she had never seen, chosen by her parents.

'And you are happy?' queried Elsie-Nora. The girl did not seem to comprehend the question. 'He is a good man, he does not drink or beat me and when our daughter was born,' (she gestured at the child standing by her) 'he was not angry. Now we have a son,' she displayed the infant with pride, his eyes kohl-rimmed, a large black spot on his face to distract malevolent spirits and ward off the evil eye, 'and he is content. He provides well for us.'

'How simple and uncomplicated,' thought Elsie-Nora, 'how marvellous to have such a clear uncluttered road to travel, to know where one is going and with whom.' When we glance casually into another's life it often appears much simpler or happier than our own because we cannot see the bends and twists that are so apparent in our own. Behind the calm of a face we cannot see private grief or longings unfulfilled.

It was then, Elsie-Nora says, that the idea came to her mind and it crystallized when faced by Robert's shifting, guilty eyes and Poddar's hooded, vulpine expression. She had decided that she would escape them all, assume her other self, become her other part and be an Indian.

From the depths of her wardrobe where it had lain hidden for so long, Elsie-Nora retrieved her sari and she wrapped herself in it. Then she waited in the living-room for her mother to appear. Constantia Ronby took a long look at her daughter and then she said: 'So, you have let him get away and y'all are going to play at being Indian again, are you? Well, my girl, I told y'all that first time and maybe I should say it again, so I'm saying it again and y'all better open your ears wide and listen well, I'll not have any Indian living in my house an'all as my daughter.'

'That, Mater, was exactly what I wanted to hear y'all say,' replied Elsie-Nora, outwardly calm but seething inwardly, for she knew they had come to a parting of the ways. 'Since that is

what you want, I am going away and I shall make a life for-
myself. I have no future here in Shahpur.' The words sounded
dramatic and artificial to her and she hoped her mother would
laugh and the matter somehow resolve itself. But Mrs Ronby
looked at her and replied: 'Y'all are a fool, my girl, I'm not sure
y'all are not a bigger fool even than our Gloria. Go where y'all
want and come back here on'y when y'all are ready to be
sensible.' It was said without heat, more in sorrow than in anger,
because Constantia Ronby had hoped for so much from her
youngest, best-looking child. In her view, Robert had been
handed to Elsie-Nora on a plate, like manna from heaven, (even
though she was not much impressed with him apart from the
fact that he was British) and Elsie-Nora had let him get away.

The die was cast. Elsie-Nora's next action was to go to the
office and hand in her notice. Mr Poddar looked at her in her
green sari and his eyes fell before hers. 'I wish you well, I'm
sure,' he said and walked away. The old Indian accountant, an
old-fashioned Marwari, handed her her dues and smiled with
pleasure at the sight of her. 'You have done well,' he said, 'I am
sure God will bless you,' and he folded his hands in a namaste
and Elsie-Nora did likewise.

She had decided to go to Delhi where her old school friend,
Vera Robins, lived; Vera had always said that there were plenty
of good jobs to be had and she had often urged Elsie-Nora to
visit her. A telegram was despatched to warn Vera of her
imminent arrival and Vera replied welcoming her and assuring
her of instant employment.

When Elsie-Nora left the house it was in silence for her
mother declared she had nothing to say to her and Mary,
genuinely affected by the departure of her nursling, wept
silently, wiping her eyes on her sari when her mistress glared at
her. Mr Ronby was away on his train and so Elsie-Nora left a
note for him explaining her action and gave it to Mary to give to
him when he returned. She did not bother to say goodbye to her
sister, Gloria and her brother-in-law, Billy.

The train journey from Shahpur to Delhi was not a long one.
Elsie-Nora sat in her second-class compartment, overcrowded as

Indian trains always are, with 'People carrying everything including the kitchen sink and making space where no space could be seen with the naked eye,' said Elsie-Nora. 'I sat there like an island amidst all that flotsam and jetsam and I tell you, m'n, I had plenty of time to think. I sat at my window and watched the familiar landmarks of Shahpur recede in the distance and I suppose I knew dimly that I would never go back, not in any real sense, and I couldn't help crying.'

She tried at first to pretend that a bit of soot from the engine had got in her eye and then she realized that nobody cared. 'It was all right to cry when one left home, a lot of the others were as well and everybody tried to cheer one another up. Indian trains are friendly places and in no time at all fellow passengers are like lifetime friends, sharing food and information. I was dressed in a sari, I was one of them, no one gave me a second look.'

The train thundered through the dusty Indian plain, whistling shrilly, full of the self-importance of an express, as it shot through little wayside stations where tired travellers looked at it with awe, bound as it was for the capital. By the time the landmarks of Delhi appeared, seeming to float in a summer dust-haze, Elsie-Nora had disappeared. It was not yet clear who was going to take her place, she had not decided on a name, although something hovered at the back of her mind, but she felt that a new name was needed to go with her new appearance, her sari-clad new self.

Vera Robins was at the station to meet her and Elsie-Nora was amused to see her friend's eyes pass without recognition over her, lost in that sari-clad throng. 'People see only what they expect to see, not what is in front of them. Sounds profound, no?' Elsie-Nora smiles.

Vera, having been hailed by Elsie-Nora, greeted her with affection but: 'Why the sari, m'n?' she asked.

'Why not, Vera, don't y'all think it looks good? We are more than half Indian, y'know, besides it's very comfortable and beats travelling in a tight skirt I can tell you.'

They hired a tonga and as they clip-clopped along in the horse-drawn carriage, Vera told Elsie-Nora of her plans. 'I have an interview for you lined up for tomorrow. It's a very good job with a big bank. I'm sure y'all'l have no trouble getting it. I've also fixed up a room for you in the YWCA, that's where I stay, so that is where we are going now.'

At the YWCA Elsie-Nora was asked to register and as she bent to sign the book, she hesitated briefly. 'Forgotten your own name, Elsie?' Vera asked laughingly.

'Yes,' was the reply, 'that's exactly what it is.' She bent once more and quickly and firmly wrote her name. Vera came to her side and looked down at what she had written and then she looked at her friend: 'What the hell's going on, m'n?' she asked in a low voice so as not to be overheard by the clerk.

'That's my new name, that's me, I am Sinara Ranbir from now on. It's only another way of saying Elsie-Nora Ronby, really. I think it's quite clever of me,' said Elsie-Nora. That was what had been at the back of her mind on the train between Shahpur and Delhi. 'I suppose so,' Vera agreed, 'but don't blame me if I go on calling you Elsie.'

Elsie-Nora was surprised at how easy it was to assume a new identity and she realized how many assumptions people make about one because of one's name. She was amused when her interviewer requested her to do an English proficiency test, something which as Anglo-Indian Miss Ronby had never been required of her, but as Indian Miss Ranbir was necessary. 'I wasn't really surprised because after the British left, India went through a whole lot of policy changes about the official language and the standard of English just went down and down, lots of young Indians coming out of school hardly able to speak it,' Elsie-Nora explains.

She got the job without any difficulty. Of course, when she showed her references she had to explain the change of name, but this proved to be no difficulty because many people were changing their names during that time. 'There were people with Muslim names who thought something less Islamic was more appropriate for Hindustan and there was our lot, Law becoming Lal, Ramsbotham becoming Rampal,' said Elsie-Nora. 'In any case, nobody else in the office knew, it was just a note in my confidential file.'

The young men and women working with her at the bank were friendly and they all accepted her as Sinara Ranbir although for some time after her arrival she was on tenterhooks lest she make some dreadful mistake and give herself away. 'It was important to me that no one knew who I really was. I wanted to start again with a clear slate as an Indian. Otherwise, it seemed to me, the whole experiment was valueless.'

Delhi was a complete change from small and claustrophobic Shahpur, a town Elsie-Nora had taken for granted as one tends to when one has been born and bred in a place. New Delhi, in the years following independence, was slowly developing an identity. It had become the capital of British India for only a few years before they departed; until then it had been Madras and Calcutta that had been favoured as the seat of colonial power, but there had been many Delhis before the English created New Delhi, many another conqueror such as the Lodhis and the Mughals had sited their capital there, as many picturesque ruins testify so eloquently.

The English fashioned New Delhi with loving care. Government House, where the Viceroy lived, was an imposing building, flanked by equally impressive official edifices hewn from red sandstone, combining the styles of India and Europe with harmony and grace. There were fine broad avenues where the English lived in large bungalows engulfed by shady gardens, far from the hurry and bustle of native areas such as Chandni Chowk (Silver Street), Daryaganj, the Jama Masjid and the Red Fort, all of them in what became designated as Old Delhi.

To some people, though not to Elsie-Nora fresh from provincial Shahpur, New Delhi seemed like an overgrown village compared to the urban, metropolitan atmosphere of established cities like Calcutta and Bombay where trade and commerce flourished and the people were more go-ahead.

'Then,' says Elsie-Nora, 'the Punjabi influx into Delhi, which began during the Partition, changed all that and gave a new identity to this very dignified government city.'

Elsie-Nora went with some trepidation to her first party as an Indian girl but also with a sense of excitement. She was beginning to lose some of her early nervousness about changing her name and her persona; there were Indians like Amanullah, one of the executives, who told her he had changed his name by deed poll to Aman Nath because he did not want to be mistaken for a Muslim which he was not.

She was not quite sure what to expect of her first social encounter. After Tarun and the Tuesday Club in Shahpur, Elsie-Nora had not had much to do with Indians. 'I felt that this party was important because it would show whether I was fully accepted in my Indian persona and so I was a bit nervous because I did not want any little slip to give me away. I did not entirely enjoy pretending to be someone else, but then I would say to myself "Who am I?" and argue that I was only giving the other half of me, or three-quarters if one is accurate, a chance to come out of hiding.'

The party was given by Rajni Mehta, one of the girls who worked in Elsie-Nora's section. There was an interesting mixture of young people, working women of all types; 'There were teachers, a lawyer, some medical students, advertising people, the first woman selected for the IAS, India's continuation of the British Indian Civil Service. I was introduced to an air-hostess, a beautiful girl, and I was intrigued to find that she was considered fast and a good-time girl because of her profession. There were quite a few lewd jokes all evening about 'layovers'! I suppose every society sets up notions of behaviour that are then knocked over like ninepins. I tell you, m'n, it was rather funny the way I, dressed in a sari (I wore nothing else those days), looked at that air-hostess who was wearing black toreador pants that left nothing to the imagination and I watched the way all the men looked at her! It was at this party that I discovered that the Indian working girl was now considered fair game. They were a new phenomenon, assertive, living alone in the big city. They had pretty well replaced us poor Anglos!'

Some of the girls, greatly daring, smoked cigarettes and this obviously set up in the minds of some who watched them, preconceptions about behaviour, smoking being considered 'fast'. Such girls were also considered 'fair game'. Why do we think of men as hunters and women as the hunted? Quite a few of the girls in that room wore western dress instead of the sari.

'When I looked round that room that evening,' Elsie-Nora said 'I couldn't help thinking of Tarla and wondering what she would have made of it, this brave new India that was evolving. Most of the young people there had come of age after independence and had few hang-ups, it seemed, about adopting what they liked from western ways. American ways, to be precise. I just sat there in my sari, pretending to be someone else, like a visitor from another planet.'

Someone sat down beside her and asked her name. Elsie-Nora stiffened in alarm for a moment before she remembered that there was nothing to fear.

'Sinara Ranbir,' she replied, decorously arranging the end of her sari over her shoulder. Her interlocutor was a nice-looking young man.

'You're Punjabi then?' Elsie-Nora nodded and then quickly asked: 'And you?'

'I'm Punjabi too,' he replied, 'My name is Chand Malhotra. I suppose you dropped the Singh at some stage.'

'I beg your pardon?'

'Ranbir Singh, that's the usual form,' he told her.

'Oh. Yes, I guess so, but it happened a long time ago so I really don't know,' Elsie-Nora said airily and felt quite pleased with herself when the young man nodded and went on to something else. She felt as though she had passed some sort of test.

It was a good feeling, Elsie-Nora reflected, as she sat with Chand Malhotra and they talked about their work, about movies and books, to be able to merge into a group, to be accepted as one of them. She realized, of course, that the moment she got close to anyone the truth would have to come out. What effect that might have she did not know. 'But right then I wasn't planning on getting close to anyone, I was just intent on getting a life of my own going,' Elsie-Nora says.

Chapter Eleven

In her hurry to create a persona, to gain credence for Sinara who had emerged full-blown, but in something of a rush, Elsie-Nora had invented a great many things without fully considering where they might lead her. To explain away the fact that she spoke no Pubjabi, and precious little Hindi either, she had invented a family abroad and this falsehood entrapped her in another when she allowed it to be assumed that her father was a diplomat.

Living as I do in London, I find it difficult to comprehend this need to have a background. Nobody here cares who your father is (or even if you don't have one), not unless you are out of the top drawer. No one your own age will spend time trying to discover who or what your parents are, it simply is not relevant to you as an individual and when it's time to marry (and not a lot of people are doing that these days), it still isn't relevant unless you choose to make it so. I was inclined to think at first that Elsie-Nora was making a bit of a fuss about nothing with all her talk about parents and where she came from, but then I remembered my father and how his family reached across the intervening ocean and took their son back unto themselves and I suppose this must be the way they carry on in India.

Elsie-Nora was afraid of intimacy with any young man, aware that it must ultimately lead to unmasking, for when it came time for families to be, as it were, exchanged, the truth must out. Then Ranbir would metamorphose back into Ronby and how then to justify the deception? 'If I was saying that being who I really am was not good enough for me, then how could I offer to someone else what I seemed to consider base coin? That is what I asked myself,' explains Elsie-Nora, 'and I knew I had got in rather deeper than I'd meant to when it all began. Anyway, because I did not encourage young men, I got the reputation for being aloof and unapproachable.'

Elsie-Nora did not immediately realize what *that* was going to involve. She had become friendly with Chand Malhotra who, when he discovered that she allowed no liberties and was too straitlaced to be what he called 'good fun', was content to be her friend and companion. He introduced her to his mother and told that lady that Sinara was a nice girl but a bit of a bore.

In a fond Indian mother's parlance this translated to 'modest' and 'well-brought up', qualities that made her desirable as a daughter-in-law. Hearing her son describe her as prim and proper, despite being a working girl away from her family and that too, one brought up in Vilayat, England, seeing her always neatly dressed in a sari, Mrs Malhotra decided that this was the girl for her son. A girl, she decided, able to keep her erratic moon boy on the straight and narrow as a good wife should.

Bulbul Malhotra might have been named for a songbird, the Indian nightingale, but she was of that species known as a social climber. Like any garden creeper, she twined herself around the stalwarts of society, climbing relentlessly to where the sun shines brightest . . . at the top. Her galaxy contained such luminaries as the prime minister's family, and she collected ambassadors of every shape, size and hue and anyone else whom the world accounted important. It pleased her that Sinara's family was 'diplomatic', living abroad, it sounded good to her snobbish ears. What she did not like so much was Sinara's singular lack of jewellery, but indulgently she put this down to the idiosyncratic ways of 'today's young people' rather than to the real reason which was, of course, that Elsie-Nora possessed none. Bulbul Malhotra made a mental note to insist that plenty of gold, diamonds and pearls formed part of the dowry, as befitted their status.

Chand had been attracted to Sinara on the very first evening they had met, but had soon found her too dull for his taste since she permitted no intimacy and did not act 'modern' like some of the other girls in his set. This perspective, however, changed when his mother began to consider her as his prospective bride. What was not alluring in a girlfriend, decorous behaviour and a strict moral code, was highly desirable in a wife.

It is the aim of every Indian male to marry a virgin, a 'good girl', his line of reasoning being that if he can have it off with a girl, who was to tell how many others might not have been before him. It is mind boggling to consider the fate of Indian girls who love not wisely but too well!

'At first,' Elsie-Nora says, 'I did not understand the veiled remarks and sentimental inuendoes that Chand kept making. I used to tell him to stop looking at me like a mooncalf (his name, Chand, means moon) and he would sigh deeply and quote some obscure Urdu poem. His favourite, I recall, was "If the mountains shrug off their mantle of snow, the valleys below see their magnificence".'

Unused to the courting rituals of the pukka Indian, she did not recognize it when applied to her. The truth only dawned when Bulbul Malhotra arrived one evening at the YWCA and began to interview her. It was only then that she realized that she, or rather Sinara whom she had created, was being sought in marriage.

There followed then a charade that would under any other circumstances have amused Elsie-Nora; now, so many years later, she smiles wryly. 'Ironical, no?' she asks, 'I toyed with the idea of playing a part in the charade, of somehow arranging it so that I could become Chand Malhotra's wife. The Partition had caused enough dislocation in the Punjab so that one could hide behind stories of lost and separated families. But I knew this would not work for me because, having placed my mythical family abroad I would have to produce them. Then would follow the question of dowry, they did not demand such big dowries in those days so there was none of this widespread wife-burning that we read about nowadays, but even so I would have had to produce a sizeable amount of money, jewellery and a trousseau to satisfy Bulbul Malhotra.'

Mrs Malhotra cut through Elsie-Nora's polite evasions like a hot knife through butter (I've always wanted to use that phrase) and demanded to know where Elsie-Nora's family could be reached. 'I know you are feeling shy, but you must tell me so that I can get in touch with them at once,' Mrs Malhotra said, her annoyance at Elsie-Nora's dilatoriness showing through her smiles.

Informed that the Ranbirs lived abroad, Bulbul Malhotra said sharply: 'Yes, yes, but they must have an address, that is what I am wanting to know from you.'

Elsie-Nora crossed herself surreptitiously and announced: 'My mother is dead and I do not see much of my father.'

'You must have other relations living?' Mrs Malhotra demanded their addresses.

Everybody in India has relatives; if not immediate family, there will be uncles and aunts and cousins, even to the nth degree. No respectable family lacks members. There may be some that need to be suppressed, such as a mad uncle or a widowed aunt who inexplicably produces a baby long after it could possibly be licit, but there are always others: 'my uncle the judge', 'my cousin the governor'.

So when Elsie-Nora stammered and stuttered and was so hopelessly out of her depth, Mrs Malhotra regarded her confusion with growing suspicion and returning home no wiser than when she had left it, she told everyone within earshot that 'there is something very strange about that Ranbir girl'. Bulbul Malhotra, however, was nothing if not determined and her blood was up; she began a systematic investigation, asking every Punjabi she knew (and her acquaintance was vast) whether anyone had 'ever heard of those mysterious Ranbirs'.

There were, of course, several Ranbirs unearthed in the course of this investigation, some of whom admitted to having relatives in England (Punjabi immigration to England was in full swing), but none of them could claim Sinara with certainty. It was not a traditional name. She would have done better with a name such as Pummy or Nimmi.

'I on'y became aware of this flurry of activity going on,' Elsie-Nora said, 'when my boss called me in and said that he had been approached about my background and credentials in a matrimonial enquiry. Having looked up my file which was, he said, singularly sparse, he had unearthed the fact that I was born in Shahpur and he told me he had so informed the Malhotras.'

Elsie-Nora now began to feel really hunted and was unable to see any humour in the situation she had created, however unwittingly, of herself as an Indian girl being sought in marriage. She knew that if Bulbul Malhotra carried her enquiries to Shahpur, to her old school, the Presentation Convent, it would soon be discovered that no Sinara Ranbir had studied there in the years she had put down on her job application form. Elsie-Nora feared that someone like Mother Josepha, now the convent's Mother Superior, but formerly her class-teacher, would soon put two and two together and guess the identity of Sinara Ranbir. The sisters at the convent all knew that Elsie-Nora had fled to Delhi.

'I wondered what to do. Ought I to own up, tell Chand the truth? I knew he was a good sport and had a sense of humour, but I knew that he would never keep the story to himself; it would soon circulate and at best I would become a laughing stock, at worst I might be ostracized by the small group of people I called my friends. I did not have the courage to face possible isolation and loneliness in a place like Delhi. My instinct was to let things ride, to wait and see if Bulbul Malhotra would get fed up and give up, but I also knew that I could not let disclosure catch me unawares.'

In her agitation, her work at the office began to suffer and her boss called her in and more in sorrow that in anger, said: 'Miss Ranbir, I realize that all these matrimonial plans must be distracting for you, but I must ask that while you remain with us you give your work at least some of your attention. If you were not normally such a good worker I would be compelled to take serious action.'

'Yes, sir, I'm very sorry, sir,' Elsie-Nora stammered, genuinely contrite, and immediately applied herself to finishing all the tasks she had allowed to accumulate.

As she sat alone that evening in her office, her backlog of typing and her filing more or less up to date, Elsie-Nora opened up her typewriter once more and typed a letter to her godmother. She had sent Mrs Graham a picture postcard from Delhi, informing her of her whereabouts and had received a letter in return in which Elinor Graham wrote of her loneliness in London, of how much she missed the good old days in Shahpur, adding that she would have welcomed a visit from Elsie-Nora, 'But,' she wrote, 'I suppose now that you have started on this new life in Delhi, you will have no wish to come to England to be with your very lonely godmother.'

Elsie-Nora wrote to remind her godmother of that letter; 'I should be very glad, if you still need me Aunt Elinor, to come and look after you for as long as you wish. I was most sorry to hear that you have not been well . . . .'

Unbeknownst to Elsie-Nora, her mother had also written to Elinor Graham. Mrs Ronby had had time to cool down and to regret her rift with her daughter. She longed for her to return home, but realized that there was little future for her in Shahpur and so she would not write asking her to return. Mary kept urging her to do it: 'House not same to same without childrens,' she wailed, ostentatiously holding her sari to her eyes, 'Why for Missy not write Missy baba tell her comes home?'

Instead, Mrs Ronby wrote to Elinor Graham who in an earlier letter had complained of being lonely and uncared for, of her children's neglect of her. She suggested that it would be very nice for poor Elinor, who was so obviously unwell and alone, to have her god-daughter come and stay with her. 'She will be like a daughter to you and a good companion for you. She is a beautiful girl and I am sure you will love her,' she wrote.

Elinor Graham might not have responded quite as readily and generously as she did had it not happened that she suffered a particularly painful attack of arthritis and that both her sons and their wives found a plenitude of reasons why they could neither have her to stay, nor spare the time to come and look after her. Overcome by exhaustion and pain as she climbed the stairs with her shopping, she then spilled hot tea over herself as she tried to pour out a nice cup of tea from the heavy Georgian teapot which seemed to reproach her for its tarnished condition. She sat down almost immediately and replied to Constantia's letter, begging her to send Elsie-Nora immediately and that she would meet all her expenses.

Cannily, giving the godmother no time to change her mind, Mrs Ronby acted with speed; she booked Elsie-Nora on the first available ship sailing from Bombay and then wrote to tell her daughter what she had done.

'At last poor old Mater was able to feel that things were going the way she wanted them to. She visited all her friends and relatives to announce with triumph that I was going Home to live, going Home for good, as she put it.'

Gloria was openly resentful: 'I don't see why she has to have all the chances an' all. Why can't it be me that has the chance to go Home, why do I have to be stuck here, I'd like to know. Y'all never do anything for me, on'y for her,' bad-temperedly she struck out at one of her children who had strayed too close.

'Well,' said Mrs Ronby, not unreasonably, 'y'all do have four children and a husband. I told y'all and told y'all till I was blue in the face, to look before y'all went and leaped, but did y'all listen to me? Listened, my foot! No, y'all had to go and get yourself in the family way and now y'all are stuck and no use blaming me an' all. Didn't I tell y'all I didn't think much of Lavvy Wilkins? I knew with a mother like that, poor Billy wouldn't be up to much, but y'all just went on having one baby after another and now you've got to make the best of a bad job,' this last said with a telling look at her son-in-law who, as usual, was eyeing the locked drink-cupboard. His frequent depredations had caused Mrs Ronby to wear the key tied firmly round her neck.

Glaring at her daughter's husband, she intoned: 'As y'all make your bed, so y'all have to lie in it.' Mrs Ronby was a regular churchgoer and loved to quote from the Bible, usually favouring the more bloodthirsty bits from the Old Testament. This scriptural injunction had the desired effect of prising Bill from the settee where he was lounging. He left the house, shouting something indistinguishable as he went. The children followed him and Gloria departed to the kitchen in a flood of tears to collect the chutneys and sauces Mary had made for her to sell.

Elsie-Nora in Delhi received her mother's letter with delight. She made her preparations for departure with celerity, allowing no time for apprehension or doubt. 'When a long-cherished dream comes suddenly within one's grasp, one cannot help being afraid that it will prove to be only a dream that vanishes on waking,' she says. 'I quickly handed in my resignation and said I was going back to England to join my family. I felt some people looked at me somewhat strangely, perhaps they had known all along that I was not what I pretended to be and had played along with me; they all knew of Bulbul Malhotra's wild-goose chase after Sinara Ranbir's elusive family.'

Chand Malhotra was desolate. Baulked of the bride he had been promised, he convinced himself that he was desperately in love and quite fancied himself in the role of the star-crossed lover. His mother had not given up her quest for Sinara's family, but it had become an academic pursuit for, as she told Chand, 'There is something very strange there, you mark my words. So much secrecy about one's family can only be because she has something to hide. I will find out what it is, never fear, but I will not let you marry her.' She did not think it necessary just then to inform him that she had secured instead the daughter of a minister with plenty of money and sets of jewellery to give his daughter. In addition, a car and a refrigerator were being negotiated by her.

Chand fancied himself in the role of a lover unjustly deprived of his beloved and he mooned around Elsie-Nora, quoting poetry, likening her eyes to darts that pierced his soul and her movements to that of *apsaras*, celestial maidens, who could seduce sages so what chance did he, a mere mortal, stand? He got so seriously in her way that Elsie-Nora, throwing caution to the winds, told him the truth about herself.

She had always liked Chand and had not liked deceiving him and anyway, she was burning her boats and felt that she had nothing to lose. Chand, when she told him, was torn between indignation at being, as he put it, 'taken for a ride' and amusement at the futile chase his mother had embarked on. He saw the humour of it all eventually and the disclosure had the desired effect of cooling his ardour as suddenly as if a cold douche had been applied.

Elsie-Nora, too, was torn between emotions of relief at being able to step back into her own self, at becoming a 'real' person again, and regret at the departure of Sinara Ranbir who, however briefly and illusorily, had been able to live at one with the country, a part of the majority for once.

Sinara would never live again and with her demise perhaps Elsie-Nora never again experienced what it was to belong. She was going to England to which she owned part of her being but which had not shaped her in any sense that ultimately matters. She was well aware, despite her mother's optimism and her own sense of excitement about going Home, that she was once more going to be the alien. As she says: 'Nobody told me that, after all, one's country is where the smell, the taste, the colour, is familiar.'

When Elsie-Nora arrived in London, having been seen off by a tearful but triumphant Mrs Ronby, a depressed-looking Mr Ronby who suddenly seemed to have shrunk, a tearful, resentful Gloria who kept seizing and smacking her offspring as they raced round the Shahpur station, it was raining. The city, blackened by soot and smog, looked dark and forbidding and as Elsie-Nora stood at last in England, the Home they had all dreamed of for so long, she saw it as a frightening blur and felt very far from home.

Chapter Twelve

Elinor Graham had been one of the *burra* memsahibs of Shahpur in the days of the British Raj, her husband Henry Graham having been Commissioner of Shahpur District. Elinor had got to know Constantia Ronby during the course of her pregnancies and had been nursed by her at the Lady Curzon Wing For Europeans where Constantia had been first a nurse, then assistant matron and finally, matron.

A memsahib of the old school, Elinor Graham had found much in common with Constantia Ronby; they both despised the Natives, seeing them as hopeless, needing to be kept at arms length. They both shared a notion of western superiority, both moral and physical. Of course, it was clearly understood that as an Anglo-Indian, Constantia was in no way Elinor's equal, but since Mrs Ronby knew her place this never presented a problem to the two of them. When Constantia gave birth to her third daughter, Mrs Graham graciously consented to be the child's godmother.

'That was yet another thing that made Gloria jealous of me,' Elsie-Nora recalls, 'I always got nicer presents than she did from her godmother. I had dolls from England, pretty frocks and once, a lovely bright red tricycle.'

Elsie-Nora remembers being taken as a child to visit her godmother at her bungalow and how awed she was by the splendour in which they lived. 'Mr Graham had been a great shikari, hunter, and the walls of every room and a great many floors were festooned with the heads and skins of tiger, lion, bear and stags of all kinds with many-branched antlers. Their eyes seemed to follow me around the room and I did not like that at all. The Grahams kept a small army of servants, the indoor servants all dressed in white with scarlet cummerbunds round their waists, starched turbans on their heads and immaculate white gloves. Outside, another battalion of retainers tended the garden, carried water, opened and shut gates and swept the grounds. There were syces for the horses and the children's ponies and there were the faceless, nameless untouchables, the sweepers, who crept in and out of the bathrooms emptying the 'thunder boxes' before water closets appeared in Shahpur and doing all the other menial tasks that the upper-class servants would not.'

One of those memsahibs who believed fervently in the 'white man's burden', Mrs Graham never considered India to be ready for independence. She cherished the idea that Indians ought to be grateful for the blessings of benevolent British rule and frequently said that only misguided Natives were not. Elsie-Nora had heard her declare often enough that Indians, like children seeking unwholesome sweets, might demand independence, but the British like wise parents must deny it to them. When, therefore, India did become independent she was like one demented by anger and grief. 'It did not help matters that her husband went and died at the very same time. Aunt Elinor always insisted that he died of a broken heart, that he gave his life to India; but in her heart of hearts,' Elsie-Nora says, 'I think she blamed him for dying when he did, leaving her alone and unable to cope.'

It was a bitter and lonely woman who finally decided that India no longer held any place for her and she returned to England, leaving behind in the cemetery at Shahpur two daughters who had died in infancy and her husband, Henry.

She had two sons in England, but the exigencies of Empire had meant that the Grahams had seen little of their sons, having sent them off at the tender age of six to boarding-school in England, far from the spoiling tendencies of tender-hearted ayahs. Now these young men in turn had no time for their mother who returned to them a querulous, unhappy woman who could not adjust to a way of life that was unfamiliar to her and who harked back constantly to bygone days.

'You could not really blame George and Gerald, Aunt Elinor's sons,' Elsie-Nora says, 'They had their own lives to lead and found their mother depressing and also, I think, somewhat embarrassing, what's that word, an anachronism?'

Unhappy in unglamorous post-war England, without friends, Mrs Graham's thoughts kept returning to India, to Shahpur, where she had been happy, had known importance, lived well. That was her country which with the stroke of a pen, Whitehall had deprived her of. None of her English acquaintance remained in Shahpur and so it was to Constantia Ronby that she turned with letters and Christmas cards, becoming a more assiduous godmother to Elsie-Nora than ever she had been in her heyday in Shahpur.

'Mater always wrote back telling her what, I suppose, she wanted to hear, how everything had gone down the drain and how "jumped-up Natives were running things now and making a mess of it all". It was what Aunt Elinor wanted to hear because it showed that she had been right all along, that Indians could not be trusted to run the country properly, that Henry Graham and men like him were what India needed. It restored something to her that at other times she felt she had lost. Sad, no?'

Usually, in the stories of once upon a time, when a fairy godmother waves her wand it converts a wretched Cinderella or a goose-girl into a princess who finds her prince and lives happily ever after. Mrs Graham, however, was a fairy godmother made bad-tempered by arthritis and filial neglect, embittered by her husband's lack of foresight and self-preservation which had stranded her in inflationary post-war England alone.

As she sank into ill-health, senility and death, Elinor Graham lived more and more in the past, in the splendours of colonial India where dozens of servants had waited on her hand and foot. As there were no servants in Camden Town, apart from a stream of 'dailies' who never lasted long, it fell to Elsie-Nora to fulfil her godmother's imperious commands.

It could be imagined that we are getting ready to leave Elsie-Nora high and dry, albeit not dry-eyed, in the hostile environment of a London she cannot adjust to. But as I said at the very beginning, it was not all gloom and doom there and Elsie-Nora never became depressed.

Whenever she could manage it she went out, often to the cinema where she lost herself in the lives of others, living their problems, enjoying their dreams; she also loved to dance and so she went often to that phenomenon now being revived, the *thé dansant* or tea dance. In those genteel dance halls many lonely people hankering for a gentler past, for remembered music, sought refuge from Teddy Boys, Mods and Rockers and their incomprehensible music and customs. England was still recovering from the deprivation of the war years and people were trying to come to terms with a world that had been stood on its head and now did not seem to have regained its feet.

It was at a tea dance that Elsie-Nora met Hugh Walker. He asked her to dance and they both found the experience enjoyable. They also discovered that they were both from India. Thereafter, it became his practice to seek her out and soon they were going out together. Hughie, as she called him, was fair-skinned, blue-eyed and fair-haired; he had spent most of his youth in India where his parents had described themselves as 'Domiciled Europeans'. Nobody seems very sure what this term meant. It does not appear in the Government of India Act, which in 1935 defined Anglo-Indians, so perhaps it is a euphemism for those who did not wish to call themselves Anglo-Indian, although many English people are also said to have called themselves 'Domiciled'.

Hugh Walker is an Anglo-Indian. Elsie-Nora never actually has come out and said that he is, only saying: 'It's nice to be with someone from a shared background, then there is no need for all those tedious explanations and footnotes like y'all get in some books.'

Hugh could well be English, but there is something about the way he speaks, oh very correct and sort of clipped, but with an intonation that sometimes reminds me of Elsie-Nora. His father had been in government service and the family had left India just before independence.

After their arrival in England Hugh lost his father and being the only son, had to take on the care of his mother who by all accounts was as big a memsahib in her way as Elinor Graham. Hugh was not in his first youth when he and Elsie-Nora met; living with an elderly and autocratic parent could not have enhanced his chances of matrimony, and from the dance she led her poor son I cannot believe that Chrystelle Walker would have struck any girl as anything but an unwelcome encumbrance.

Because of Mrs Graham, Elsie-Nora was not free to marry and Hughie had his mother to take care of, so for quite a while after they met, their meetings had to be confined to dance halls and cinemas when they could leave their charges in the care of the welfare services or with a kindly neighbour.

'Once and only once,' Elsie-Nora remembers, 'we plucked up the courage to meet in Regents Park and each of us brought along mother and godmother. We had hoped that the two old ladies would hit it off and pave the way to Hughie and me getting married, which is what we wanted to do.' Elsie-Nora laughed, 'Sadly, it was quite the opposite. Aunt Elinor was in a more than usually imperial mood that day and she imagined she was back in India, something that was happening more and more often as she became senile. She kept seeing snakes in the park and when Hughie and his mother appeared she played the *burra* Memsahib, the Commissioner's lady, to the hilt.'

From the way she behaved to the Walkers it must be deduced that with her unfailing memsahib instinct she had sussed out that they were Anglo-Indians. While Constantia Ronby had been her friend, it had always been on her terms: she had never allowed Mrs Ronby to suppose she was her equal and Constantia had known her place. Obviously, Chrystelle Walker did not and Mrs Graham was outraged by her presumption.

'This country,' she remarked to Elsie-Nora, 'has come to a pretty pass when anybody thinks they can claim one's acquaintance.' The two ladies were seated side by side on a bench and Mrs Graham, ignoring Mrs Walker, spoke over her head to Elsie-Nora.

'I never did condone rudeness,' Mrs Walker said grandly to her son, 'I am not going to start now. Let us go home, son.'

142

'Look out, woman,' was Elinor Graham's response, 'there is a cobra not an inch from your foot. Give me my cleft stick, Devi Lal, I'll soon deal with the creature.' Devi Lal was her major domo in Shahpur.

Chrystelle Walker, who used a walking-stick, did the nearest thing to a leap that she could manage and elicited this comment from Mrs Graham: 'Never can trust a Native in a crisis.'

Elsie-Nora says the two old ladies took so violently against each other that any further meeting between them had to be ruled out. It also put paid to any idea that Elsie-Nora and Hughie might get married. What would happen to Mrs Graham if they did? She had quarrelled with both her sons and their wives who now no longer came to see her, making her Elsie-Nora's sole responsibility.

Constantia Ronby with characteristic firmness, exhorted her daughter to consign Elinor to an old people's home ('the best possible thing for her') and advocated that Hugh did likewise with his mother ('or else she'll be a millstone round your neck').

Having received a photograph of Hugh and Elsie-Nora, she was well-pleased by his appearance and bemoaned her daughter's lack of resolution which stood in the way of that long-awaited wedding.

'Gloria and Billy have put Lavvy Wilkins in a Home for the Aged,' she wrote, 'and not before time. She's quite happy there and all.'

Elinor Graham and Chrystelle Walker, of course, saw the whole thing in quite another light. They saw the romance as a threat to their happiness and security; both of them dreaded the idea of being put in a Home where their self-importance and sense of identity would not survive. Each, therefore, made it as difficult as possible for the young people to meet. Both of them used self-pity to the full to make Elsie-Nora and Hughie feel guilty, unable to enjoy each other's company.

Families! Who would ever want them and yet, who would be without? Be that as it may, emotional blackmail, ('I know I'm just a useless old woman whom you want to get rid of'), and martyrdom, ('You go off and enjoy yourself, don't worry about me, I may be dead by the time you return'), were the order of the day at 119 Morrington Terrace and at 17 Margaret Road.

Somehow, despite all this, Elsie-Nora and Hugh managed to meet, but they were unsatisfactory meetings stolen while the two old women napped, or snatched in shops like Marks and Spencer while they did the shopping.

'Imagine if you can,' says Elsie-Nora, 'having to pour your heart out while prodding a lettuce, or letting one's fingers meet in the depths of a chilled cabinet! It was,' she remembers with a smile, 'much worse when we had to meet in the butcher's shop, surrounded by all those hanging carcasses, the smell of blood and Mr Griggs the butcher in his bloodstained apron, pushing between us to get the kidneys which Mrs Walker loved, enough to put you off anything, even love. Mind you,' she adds with her cheerful laugh, 'it would have been a sight worse in the market at Shahpur, no white tiles and aprons there!' Perhaps it was a comfort that her love affair was at least conducted under hygienic conditions.

So matters went on with neither old lady showing any sign of giving in nor, and one must suppose the idea crossed their minds, of dying and leaving their young folk in peace. It must have been about this time that Elinor Graham made yet another will, this time leaving everything to Elsie-Nora, but only on condition that she was unmarried and living at 119 Morrington Terrace when her godmother died.

Mrs Graham had made more wills than some people have had hot dinners as the saying goes. She had always used her last will and testament as an instrument to beguile and threaten, first her children and then Elsie-Nora. I suppose one cannot blame the old lady, Elsie-Nora certainly did not, because her possessions were all she had left. Youth, beauty, love, status, all had deserted her, as had her children and she had to use what she had left: her house and her little remaining money. Of course, having made that will she did not conveniently die, she lingered on, ever fearful of being left alone at the end.

Mrs Walker, too, clung tenaciously to life and constantly begged her son not to desert her in her old age.

Meanwhile, Hugh and Elsie-Nora grew older and Hugh stopped counting his grey hairs because suddenly they had become too plentiful and as they stood and watched their springtime depart, so the spring went out of their step. Meeting in the shops was not much fun when one was weighed down by shopping that strained one's arms and shoulders and when one's legs ached from too much walking. The only escape was when they managed to get to the cinema and were able to sink gratefully into the comfortable seats, temporarily freed of shopping and laundry, able to hold hands, Elsie-Nora to rest her head on Hughie's shoulder and for then, to dream a little.

The only ray of hope about this cat and mouse game that the old ladies played with them was that time was not on their side. If Hughie was becoming grey and stooped a little, if Elsie-Nora complained of twinges of sciatica, consider what was happening to Elinor and Chrystelle. In their enemity it seemed as if they had entered into a contest to see who would grow old faster. Every pain and wrinkle of the one was more than matched by the other and while they pretended indifference to each other's existence, each asked surreptitious questions to elicit the state of the other's well-being or lack of it. Perhaps this gave them a reason to stay alive, added sauce to the monotony and pains of old age, so that for a time it looked as if they were set to live forever, if only so as to outlive the other. But even malice cannot keep you alive indefinitely and so it came about that one winter evening Elinor Graham put down the pack of cards with which she was attempting to play Patience, dropped her chin on her chest and died.

Hughie brought his mother to the funeral where she sat in her wheelchair, criticized the priest for his extreme youth which she seemed to take as a personal affront, turned up her nose at the wreaths and utterly despised the funeral baked meats.

Perhaps to show how much better it could be done, or because the death of Elinor had somehow dislodged something that had propped her up, or perhaps sitting in the graveyard on that bitter February day had given her a mortal chill, Chrystelle Walker also departed this life a month later.

Elsie-Nora and Hughie were free at last to marry. They did so quietly at the Registry Office, without any of the bridal trappings that once Elsie-Nora had dreamed of. None of her family was present, Constantia Ronby had died a short while before and Gloria and Bill had put Mr Ronby in the Home with Lavvy Wilkins.

'I have come full circle, I suppose,' says Elsie-Nora. 'I attempted to be Indian, had hoped to be English, had come Home and now returned to my Anglo-Indian roots by marrying Hughie. I've had a happy life and nothing counts but that. Sadness is like pain, you never remember it afterwards.'

Chapter Thirteen

Epilogue

Elsie-Nora was happy with her Hughie. She had, as she says herself, come full circle and through her marriage had gone back to her Anglo-Indian roots, yet had achieved her dream of coming Home. By the time I came on that scene, Hugh seemed an old man to me, a little sickly, so I did not see too much of him, although he was very interested in 'the book' and loved to discuss it with me.

Sometimes his mind was apt to wander a little and then he seemed to mistake me for someone else, he spoke as if I was their daughter. I suppose appearance-wise, I could very well have been, perhaps that is why Elsie-Nora welcomed me and talked so freely of her life.

I have been sheepdog to Elsie-Nora's life, shepherding her memories into the fold of this book. Some probably went astray, while others were rescued from the brink of oblivion. All of it has made me think a great deal about why people are the way they are and despite what we might like to believe, nothing has changed all that much. In England every second word you read or hear seems to have something to do with racism.

I have concentrated on Elsie-Nora's story and tried through it to portray a society that has vanished, the prejudices of that time, but also to show (I hope) that in fact nothing changes as much as we might think or hope it has. Like 'new lamps for old', we merely exchange old fears, dislikes and suspicion for others that seemingly bright and new-minted, are fashioned from old metal.

I have thought a great deal about what happened all those hundreds of years ago when east met west, when it all began. I am fascinated by what Tarla Sen said to Elsie-Nora: 'Our whole (Indian) viewpoint has changed. We cannot think purely as Indians any more, we feel with their prejudice, think with their ideas and speak with their tongue. We are dispossessed and there can be no going back.'

Even today, when so much has happened and the world has changed and changed again, that basic resentment remains in one form or another and it divides brown and black from white. That is one side of it. There is another. The western or white side.

Some recent psychological research has suggested that the white man sub-consciously associated the dark skin with excrement, 'the unwanted thing'. Which was why the people of Asia and Africa were often characterized by adjectives of uncleanliness. Horatio Ronby told Robert Grant that English people had never wanted to travel in a railway compartment with natives: 'The presence of a Native in the same carriage with you doubles the disgust one feels for a long hot journey.' This, surely, was not merely a question of conqueror and conquered, this deep-rooted dislike and distaste?

Hughie once said to me: 'This dislike you speak of may have been the result of dissociation from the familiar which increased the English awareness of India and Indians as uncongenial. After all,' he argued and I must say I was impressed by him that day, 'the Englishman must have felt out of place in India and so he reacted against it.'

India 'called' and then alienated, leaving the Englishman isolated, 'a scanty pale-faced band in the midst of millions of unfriendly vassals.' I have a theory (actually, I have several and I'm putting them all higgledy-piggledy into this last chapter) based on something I read while working on Elsie-Nora's story, that the English in India in those long-ago days lived in a sense in a return to childhood, a time when one is often afraid, dependent on others and insignificant. Take for instance, the Graham household in Shahpur with its army of servants, where the family dog had a servant of his own and the children a 'boy' to carry their bits and pieces. It was all necessary to create an impression of superiority, but it engendered dependence.

There is a flavour of unreality about it all, as someone said: 'The strong flavour of Gilbert and Sullivan . . . lay at the back of it.' Yet much in India engendered fear; fear that 'the dark horde' might at any time rebel; proper English ladies feared the harsh

Indian sun since the 'merest hint of the tarbrush is sufficient to create a stigma'. An odd mixture of fears, creating a miasma.

One way to stave off one's fears and inadequacies was to denigrate the Indian race, thus reducing the enemy to simply an unworthy opponent, an object of contempt or pity, the white man's self-imposed burden. Elsie-Nora says comfortably: 'English colonialism has shaped the world's politics and the way the world is today.' This is true.

The memory can be deceptive and human nature being what it is, most of us adjust the events of the past to show ourselves in the best possible light while the rest remains in shadow. It can be like a forest fire which blazes up, destroying much, so that all that remains is ash, through which one must sift painstakingly and with an expert's tools. After her initial surprise that anyone should want to write about her, 'nothing wonderful ever happened to me', I think Elsie-Nora enjoyed reliving her past; but just as one adjusts one's face to meet the faces that we meet, why not our memories.

My prof still mutters on about the *Jewel In the Crown*, but like I said at the very beginning, how could I? That India, the jewel in the crown, was not my India, nor am I of those who plucked it and placed it in the crown, just as I and mine have had no hand in taking it out again. In any case, I said to the prof as he looked disgruntledly at my mass of manuscript, plenty has been written about all that and enough shown on our television screens to satisfy the largest appetite for nostalgia.

Elsie-Nora and the Ronbys bring out a small corner of that world, less known, brushed aside by both the main protagonists. Yet, as Hughie said in one other blinding flash of brilliance: 'The Anglo-Indian has struggled through wrongs sufficient to crush out of existence most races. That we today retain the essential traits, instincts and culture of our forefathers, is remarkable testimony to the virility of the British nation. If England is the land of our fathers, India is the land of our mothers.' He then quoted for me an Anglo-Indian poet: 'O England! Who are these if not thy sons?'

Elsie-Nora smiles. 'It doesn't matter any more, though it used to hurt that very few people seem to know (or care) what is meant by the term Anglo-Indian. After all, every generation has to accept that much of what was important to them is meaningless or unknown to the succeeding ones.'

She strives no longer to be either one thing or the other and for that present-day London is the right place. In the melting-pot that is Camden Town, she does not stand out in any way to merit unwelcome attention (except perhaps from the drunks and derelicts who lie about the tube station and they are impartial in their insults). 'I can be myself,' she says, 'whatever I perceive that to be.'

So this is where I will leave Elsie-Nora, with her Hugh in north London. For myself, I discovered the India that gave rise to me (I know that sounds a mite pompous, but you know what I mean) and while I liked some of it, I know that I must reject the rest. I can only be myself, and having realized that, I too am at peace, no longer feeling divided from my mother and her husband. I won't go so far as to say I love him, but he's all right really and if he makes my mum happy then, as far as I'm concerned, he's fulfilling his function in life.

My grandmother, who does not approve of all this scribbling as she calls it, is inclined to think there is something wrong with me. Here comes the prejudice again, but because I have an Indian father she feels that in some strange way my antecedents are unknown and with dangerous propensities. Absorbed in my writing, I haven't backchatted her as much as is usual and so she imagines I must be wasting away from some mysterious consumptive disease. 'Too much Greta Garbo,' I tell her, but: 'After all, who knows?' she says in a whisper to my mum. I would have stuck out my tongue, but for two pins she would stick a thermometer under it or examine it for decay. She contents herself with bringing me innumerable cups of tea. 'A nice cuppa?' she asks and I nod. I suppose I must be British after all.